The

Awakening of

Ivy Leavold

Sierra Simone

To Laurelin, who asked me to write a sexy book.

And to the girls at the retreat, who gasped in all the right places.

AUTHOR NAME

Cover by Date Book Designs 2014

ISBN-13:
978-1502781000

ISBN-10:
150278100X

Chapter One

"Almost to Stokeleigh," the driver told me. "Markham Hall isn't far beyond that."

The clatter of hooves and wheels on the road prevented me from answering. Instead, I continued to watch the landscape roll by outside, thick woods and shallow vales punctuated by narrow streams and low stone bridges. Dusk fell quickly; by the time I had marked the long shadows and impenetrable murk growing between the trees, dark orange and purple streaked the sky. And by the time the carriage rolled through the small hamlet, it was almost completely dark. Only the faintest lavender remained in the night sky—the last breath of daylight—and against it was the silhouette of a house, large and tall, with a square tower at one end. It sat on a hill high above the vale of Stokeleigh, the only space cleared of trees for as far as the eye could see.

"Markham Hall," the driver shouted. I nodded, even though he couldn't see me.

I busied myself with straightening the pleats on my skirt and checking my hair. I'd never been to Markham Hall, and it had been many years since I'd been to any house as fine as this. Seven years, in fact.

The carriage stopped and the driver hopped down to open the door. I climbed out with his help, and a servant emerged from the house, helping the driver unload my single trunk and bag.

"Is this all?" the servant grunted.

"Appears that way," said the driver.

Seven years without parents had taught me to accept frugality, to be proud of it in a strange way, but now that my brother was also dead, I was in the strange position of being poor *and* at the mercy of strangers. When my cheeks burned, they burned not for the single battered trunk, but for the entirety of this situation. If the solicitor responsible for dispensing my brother's meager estate hadn't been able to track down Mr. Markham, my late cousin's husband, I would have been forced to apply for a position as a governess with some family or another. Solicitor Wickes had made the owner of Markham Hall sound like the proper old country gentleman, twice widowed and mourning the loss of his young wife, but that didn't make the prospect of accepting his kindness any less daunting. I may have been frugal, but I was also proud and used to being solitary, to claiming my time as my own. Lodging with a lonely old man sounded like its own kind of work.

"This way," the servant said, and I followed him to the entrance, a massive stone arch set with two ancient-looking doors. Black bands of iron bound the door together and the knocker was a snarling bear of tarnished brass. "Inside," he said.

The entranceway was nearly as black as the outdoors—more so, for there were no stars here. I blinked owlishly while the servant manhandled the door shut again. The driver spoke softly to the horses and the carriage rattled away.

Wait! I wanted to shout. *Don't leave me here!*

But it was too late. The carriage was gone, the door closed and I was alone in the dark. I heard the grunt and shuffle of the servant lugging my trunk somewhere.

"Where should I—"

"The housekeeper will come for you. Soon."

So, I waited in the dark, shifting my weight from foot to cold foot, suppressing my irritation at being made to wait like a stranger and at the overall lack of hospitality Markham Hall seemed to present in general. *You're only* technically *family,* I reminded myself. *Be grateful that Mr. Markham offered you a roof over your head at all...*

A dim glow appeared—a bobbing, flickering glow—and as it came closer, it was clear that it was attached to a rather severe figure dressed in black. The telltale ring of keys jangled at her hip.

"You must be Miss Leavold."

I made a low curtsey and was about to deliver my prepared speech of gratitude, but she was already turning away, shoes clicking sharply on the floor. A spike of indignation at her rudeness shot through me, but like my brother had always implored, I kept my mouth shut. Silently, I followed her.

The lamp she carried only illuminated the barest glimpses of the house. A grim tapestry here, a frowning portrait there. We climbed the wide staircase.

"I'm sorry for the lack of light," she said, not sounding sorry at all. "When Mr. Markham is away, we generally keep early hours. We are not used to having guests so late."

"I apologize for my lateness too. Though we set off before dawn, it's still a long drive." I was keenly aware that I didn't sound sorry, but I did not care. I didn't see how the hour of my arrival was any more my fault than the hour of the sun setting.

She unlocked a room and led me inside. No fire had been lit and from the damp smell, I supposed it hadn't been aired out either. I certainly didn't mind diminished conditions—it appeared to be my lot in life, after all—but one glance at the housekeeper's pinched face told me that this discomfort had been deliberately calculated.

Determined to undermine whatever trap she had laid, I declared as cheerfully as I could, "What a lovely room. I am so grateful for your care and effort."

She made a noise that indicated nothing other than an acknowledgement that I'd spoken. "Owain brought your things up already. We've long since supped, but if you feel it necessary, you can rouse the cook from her bed to tend to you."

Of course, that wasn't a real option. I made a demurring sound.

She continued. "Breakfast is early here, perhaps around six-thirty, although Mr. Markham generally eats later, perhaps around ten. I *suppose* there might be a chance that you are asked to dine with him." She sniffed, letting me know what she thought of this supposition. "He is away f**Word did not find any entries for your table of**

8

contents.requently, and I am very busy tending to the house. There are no other residents here, so you will need to occupy yourself or walk to Stokeleigh if you cannot."

She didn't know of the years I'd spent alone in my dead parents' house, with no one except the servants to keep me company, while my brother gambled away the last of our money in London. Years spent roaming the countryside, sitting by the sea, reading all the ancient books in the library. And besides, at nineteen I was no longer a child.

"I will endeavor to amuse myself," I said. "As I have done since I reached adolescence."

Another sniff. "Well. Good night then."

"Good night, Mrs…?"

"Brightmore."

She left, and by the thin trickle of moonlight, I found matches and a lamp by my bedside, which I lit. But despite the long journey and the protracted weeks of grief and uncertainty since my brother's passing, I couldn't sleep. I didn't care that it was dark as pitch and that the servants were abed—I wanted to see more of this Northern house that I would call home.

I shed my cloak and bonnet and left my room, careful to tread as quietly as possible. While I didn't think there would be anything improper about me walking about the house, I felt certain that Mrs. Brightmore would disapprove.

My corridor was lined with similar doors, all closed and presumably locked, so I went downstairs with my lamp instead. The yellow pool of lamplight did little to drive back the shadows, but I still made my tentative way into the receiving rooms of the first floor. First to the dining room, dominated by a large table and a massive iron chandelier, then to the drawing room, filled with more feminine furniture, armchairs and chaises of a lavender damask, all of it looking almost black in the darkness. In the far corner of the drawing room hung a large portrait set into an elaborate gilded frame. I walked closer and lifted the lamp. It was my dead cousin, Violet Leavold.

Violet Markham. She would have been Violet Markham when she died.

We'd met only twice, in those dreamy, peaceful years when my parents had still been alive. She'd been a few years older than me, and I vividly remembered how worldly and feminine her fourteen years had seemed to my ten the first time she'd visited. She had stayed the summer, and in those months, I had become convinced that there was no girl brighter or more lovely or more knowledgeable than Violet. The second time she came, I was twelve, and she came with the secret knowledge that only girls of sixteen had, knowledge of men and of dancing and of what happened in the secret corners of ballrooms. I'd been fascinated.

But we hadn't spoken since that last summer—not a visit, not even a letter. She had gone on to live the life befitting a beautiful girl of means and I had gone on to live like a wild thing, alone and strange

10

and wary.

Her yellow hair seemed like burnished gold in the lamplight and the portraitist had managed to capture the preternaturally blue eyes that had always seemed so daring, so bold. A gauzy shawl revealed ivory shoulders and a long, elegant neck. The blue silk gown revealed a small but shapely bust and a slender waist. Even rendered in paint, Violet's beauty and glamour were unmistakable. Life and fertility and vibrancy radiated from every curve and line of her body.

And she was dead.

"I'm sorry," I whispered to her. Thrown from her horse, the solicitor had said. And I hadn't even known that she'd gotten married. *And to think, there might be a portrait of another dead wife in this house...* I shivered.

I turned to leave and found myself face to face with someone in the dark.

Chapter Two

"Mrs. Brightmore..." My voice trailed off. It was patently not Mrs. Brightmore. It was someone tall and trim and most definitely male.

"Not Mrs. Brightmore," the man said, echoing my thoughts. I raised the small lamp, throwing his face into the light. A square jaw, straight nose, clear green eyes. Dark stubble and tousled hair told me that he'd been traveling, but the silk waistcoat and well-worn riding boots told me that he was a gentleman.

He had to be Mr. Markham, yet surely the country gentleman Solicitor Wickes had described was much, much older.

"Pardon me," I said. Apology always seemed like the best course of action. "I was having trouble sleeping and..."

He didn't answer. He walked over to a low buffet in the corner and rang a bell. A quiet but uncomfortable minute followed where I wondered if I should speak again, if I was in some sort of trouble, and then Mrs. Brightmore appeared, holding her own lamp with her bloodless mouth already puckered in rage. She saw me first and her eyes narrowed, clearly assuming that it had been me who had roused her so imperiously from her bed, but then the gentleman stepped into the lamplight.

"Mr. Markham!" she exclaimed. "But we weren't expecting you home until next week."

"Change of plans," he said shortly. His voice had a hint of a rasp to it, a huskiness that set it apart from the normally smooth and polished voices one heard in large houses. Only the barest trace of a Yorkshire accent spoke to his roots here in Dalby Forest. "A fire, Mrs. Brightmore. Supper too."

"Of course, sir," she said. "Cook is probably asleep and we dined several hours ago…"

"I'll wait," he said.

"Yes, sir." With a serrated glance at me, she left the doorway.

Within minutes a fire was lit by a servant, a handsome young man I hadn't seen before. He smiled at me before he left the room. Mr. Markham poured himself a glass of port at the buffet.

"Care for a drink?"

A lady would say no. But I'd spent these last years unchaperoned and as my own mistress, drinking brandy in bed and hauling bottles of champagne into treetops so I could taste the sweet fizz at sunset. I was accustomed to drinking, and on a chilly night in an unfamiliar house, a glass of port sounded like perfection.

"Yes, please," I said. He turned to pour another glass and then handed it to me without a word. There was no judgment or reprobation in his face, but there was something. Curiosity, perhaps.

He settled himself in a chair across from me, his long legs stretched out, his face reflective. "I imagine you are my late wife's cousin."

Here was my chance to get it done and over

with, the great thanking endeavor, which my lack of social grooming almost ensured I'd be clumsy at. Yet it had to be done. "Yes, sir—"

"Don't *sir* me," he said darkly.

"I apologize—"

"Don't do that either. Are you Ivy Leavold or not?"

"Yes, Mr. Markham. And I wanted to give you my most sincere thanks—"

"I don't want your thanks. This is not going to be an easy place for a young woman to live. It's dark and hardly modern, and I'm afraid that grief and isolation have turned me into a creature of baser needs, not capable of entertaining young ladies and certainly not capable of polite company."

I wasn't sure what to say to that. "My condolences for your loss."

He leaned forward suddenly, eyes glittering like glass. I noticed his port was drunk; I raised mine to my lips and savored the sweet, spicy taste. "Did you know her well?" he asked. "My late wife?"

"No."

He leaned back in his seat. "I see."

"We met as girls. I remember her being lovely and...vivacious." That was the kind word for girls who smoked cigars and kissed village boys, right?

He stood abruptly, going to pour himself another glass of port. "Vivacious. Yes. She was that."

"Mr. Markham, please allow me to express my gratitude for your hospitality. Were it not for your kind offer, I would have nowhere to go."

"No other family at all?"

"There was talk of a half-aunt in India, but she never answered our letters and it wasn't known if she was even still living. At any rate, I'd never met her and she didn't know me from Eve. I don't know that she would have taken me in even if she were still alive."

He sat again. "So you would have had to work."

No sense in dissembling. "Yes."

"As a governess?"

"Yes."

"And would you have detested it?"

I took another sip. "Yes. But not for the reason you are thinking. I am not afraid of work. But I am afraid of being trapped."

"Trapped?"

I made to answer, but then Mrs. Brightmore entered in again, clad in a nicer, newer dress. In the better light, I could see that she was younger than I originally supposed; like Mr. Markham, she seemed to be in her early or mid-thirties. It was the severity of her face and mien that made her seem so like the middle-aged housekeepers from the dour modern novels that my brother had loved to read.

"Supper is ready, sir," she said.

"I'll take it in here." Mr. Markham kept his eyes on me the entire time he spoke. For some reason, I felt pinned by that gaze, unable to move or look away.

"But, sir—"

"In here, Mrs. Brightmore."

She glared at me, as if Mr. Markham's dinner preferences were somehow my fault, and left in a swish of starched fabric.

I found my port glass refilled.

"So, Miss Leavold. You would feel trapped by employment?"

"I didn't mean to make myself sound indolent. It's only that I'm used to keeping my own hours, my own company. Having my life be at the whim of another's would be almost unbearable."

"And yet there are those who find more solace in imprisonment than they ever have in freedom."

"Show me such a person," I protested, then stopped. Here I was, only a few moments into meeting my benefactor, and I was contradicting him in precisely the sort of way that used to vex Thomas so.

"Is not marriage like this? Strictures and bindings that can become pleasurable?"

"Are you comparing love to imprisonment, Mr. Markham?"

Something stirred in his eyes.

"For some, perhaps." He reached across the low table between us and grasped my wrist. His fingertips were surprisingly rough for a gentleman, but the feeling of them against the thin skin of my wrist left me agitated somehow, as if he had trailed hot coals across my flesh instead of his fingers.

"Here," he said quietly, "I have your wrist

captured in my hand. You cannot move it unless I let you, you cannot touch it unless I let you. Complete confinement. But…" His fingertips made light circles—swirls, eddies—around my wrist, skipping lightly over the pale blue veins and the delicate tendons, drifting from my palm to the edge of my sleeve. He slowly unbuttoned the buttons of my sleeve, sliding it up past my elbow. Gooseflesh rose on my arms, on my neck, even on my breasts under the thin wool of my dress. It felt so close to being undressed, to being exposed.

His fingers continued their work all while he stared intently at me. "And how does this constraint feel now, Miss Leavold? If I allowed you to withdraw your wrist now, would you?"

"No," I said, my breathing coming faster. "I would not."

He bent low, as if to study my wrist, except his mouth was so near my skin, and then I was suddenly aware of my pulse pounding, of my lips parting, of the flush that was spreading on my face.

"Your dinner, sir," Mrs. Brightmore said, entering the room. The handsome servant wheeled a tray behind her, and the covered silver dishes and glassware rattled as he rolled it across the thick carpet to the armchair where his master sat. Mr. Markham didn't let go of my wrist at first—I tugged and he arched an eyebrow and I tugged again and he finally let it drop.

Relief thrummed through me. And disappointment.

17

"Is there anything else, sir?" the housekeeper inquired. Her words dropped like acid, singeing the air as they fell.

Mr. Markham ignored her, staring at me instead. She left after a minute, her quick footsteps and irritated manner making her feelings clear. *Why does she hate me so much?*

The servant winked at me before he left.

Mr. Markham opened his mouth to speak again, and then shut it, his eyes alighting on something behind me.

"Are you hungry, Miss Leavold?"

I wasn't, strangely. I felt too agitated to eat.

"I am not."

He rubbed at his forehead. "Then you should go to bed," he said.

"Sir?"

"I told you not to *sir* me, at least not now. Get to bed. The hour is too late for young women to be about. Even those accustomed to keeping their own hours."

I dearly wanted to protest. I never retired before midnight at home. But I reminded myself that *home* had been sold to satisfy my brother's grasping creditors. Markham Hall was my home now. I would do well to make myself pleasing to my cousin's widower, no matter how much I inwardly thrashed against it.

But perhaps I would grow used to it. What had he said? *Strictures and bindings that become pleasurable…*

I unconsciously touched my wrist. "Goodnight, Mr. Markham."

He didn't answer, and it wasn't until I lay in bed, watching the candlelight flicker on the ceiling, that I remembered what had been directly behind me in the parlor. The painting of my cousin Violet.

His dead wife.

Chapter Three

When I arose, I dressed myself in a gown of pale green lawn, a dress I'd always liked because it set off my olive-tinged skin and dark eyes. I was no beauty like Violet—yet properly attired, I was passable. My hair was thick and glossy and as dark as the darkest woods shipped in from India and Africa. My jaw and cheekbones were fine enough, although marred by my nose, which was slightly bumped in the middle, as my brother's had been. And my eyes were rather too large, I felt, too large and too well-rimmed by my eyelashes. For better or for worse, the darkness of my eyes and the cast of my skin—gifts from my Welsh mother—barred me from being truly considered beautiful in the pale, rosy manner of most English girls.

I went downstairs for a quiet breakfast—toast and eggs by myself in the dining room, the early morning light slanting in through the single small window. Markham Hall was brighter during the day, but it would never be an airy place. Something of a medieval gloom clung to the corners and crannies, even in the face of oncoming sunshine.

I liked it quite a lot, actually.

"Mr. Markham left for business in Scarborough early this morning," Mrs. Brightmore informed me as curtly as possible. "I have no idea when he'll be back, so you'd best not plan on his company today."

"As we discussed last night, I shall find myself

more than capable of coping on my own." Around her, politeness came only with a struggle. I resisted the temptation to demand the source of her ire with me—likely she would deny it and then resent me all the more. Better to let her fester in whatever imagined disadvantage I had put her at, while I continued on unfettered by her rancor.

After breakfast, I decided on a stroll around the grounds. Despite the melancholy air of the shadowed hall, the grounds in full summertime were wondrous, green and fresh and dappled with sunlight. I made my way past the small garden and stables and into the woods themselves, following a winding path that eventually opened into a wide pasture.

The servant from last night knelt near the dry stone wall, several cracked stones around his feet. I'd planned on a quiet morning with only myself and the trees, but I found I wanted to know more about this place that was to be my home, and so far, he'd been the only kind face I'd seen. Mr. Markham had been fascinating—magnetic even—but kind?

No. Nothing about that stern face and lean frame belied kindness.

"Hello," I said as I approached the servant.

He wiped his forehead. "Hello, miss."

"I don't think I caught your name last night. I'm Ivy Leavold, Mr. Markham's cousin by marriage."

"I'm Gareth," he said with a smile. He had an open face, blue-eyed and friendly, and when he extended his hand, I shook it. "I'm Mr. Markham's valet."

"Are valets here normally in the habit of repairing walls?"

He laughed. "Well-spotted. I was hired on as a valet three years ago, but as Mr. Markham is rarely at home—and these days prefers to travel without a servant—I've been applied to other tasks. But I shoulder my duties as best I can. It is much better than working on a farm or in a mill like my brothers."

"Yes, I suppose it is." I sat on an intact portion of the wall, staring at the verdant, rustling forest around me. At home, on a day like this, I would have run barefoot across the field or shouted until my voice grew hoarse. A wild energy then threatened to spill over into me, out of me. I wanted to feel the grass on my feet and the wind on my face and read in the sun with a bottle of Madeira nearby.

Like I would have at home.

Home.

"…careful," Gareth was telling me.

I brought myself back to the present. "My apologies," I said. "What were you saying?"

Gareth pulled some hearting stones out of a nearby pail. "I said the locals think Markham Hall is cursed. Or rather, that Mr. Markham himself is cursed. It was so awful what happened to Violet, killed only a month after they married." He spoke her name with a softness that bordered on reverence.

"Yes," I murmured, my mind drifting from this valet's familiarity with my cousin to her untimely death. "And she was such a talented horsewoman."

"It was Mr. Markham's horse," he said, and there was real pain in his voice. "She wasn't used to riding him."

Even as a girl, she'd loved riding, insisting on it every day, even in the rain. And most of all she'd loved the unpredictable horses—the stallions and the angry mares. Perhaps her death was not that shocking after all, if she still rode animals like that.

"What happened to Mr. Markham's first wife?" Gareth shrugged. "It was before I came here. Mr. Markham was a very young man when he first married, and I believe his bride was young too. She was taken with consumption, or so the stories go. Bedridden not long into their honeymoon, and died before it ended. Her grave is next to the other Mrs. Markham's, in the village churchyard."

The turrets of the tower cragged darkly over the trees. I tried to imagine the churchyard beyond the hall, no doubt as ancient and stately as the house itself. "Hard to believe such a beautiful place could see so much sadness."

"It's more beautiful on the outside than on the inside." There was a darkness to his voice, a bitter wariness, but when I glanced over at him, the source was unapparent. And I got the distinct feeling that I wouldn't learn any more from Mr. Markham's valet today.

I slid off the wall, brushing crumbled lichen off my dress. "Goodbye, Gareth."

He touched his forehead and turned back to his

work.

The path continued into the woods, trees swallowing up the pasture and the memory of Gareth as if they'd been nothing more than fairy dreams. The further I ventured in, the more fluid time felt. I could have been in Sherwood Forest during the time of King Richard or about to stumble onto a Druid rite. Only the crenellated tower through the trees reminded me of where I was, of whom I was, of my circumstances and the strange man I owed my new livelihood too.

Mr. Markham. Last night had been so unaccountable, so different from anything I'd ever experienced. He had none of the stiffness and decorum I'd experienced in wealthy gentleman, but he was hardly friendly; there was something forbidding about him that held informality at bay. Even I, lacking social graces as I did, recognized that about him. His strength came not from his station in life or his wealth, but from something else. His physicality? His self-assurance?

Whatever it was, it was impossibly alluring. Captivating. When he had held my wrist, when he had deftly unbuttoned my sleeve…I touched the smooth underside of my wrist, imagining the firelight on his face as he had talked of prisons and pleasure.

A stream bubbled nearby, purling and gurgling its way down the slope, and I stepped through a blanket of bluebells to get to the water. The water looked cool and inviting, pure and happy, and on this uncommonly warm May day, I wouldn't deny myself the pleasure of dabbling my toes in the brook. I sat and unlaced my boots, pulled off my stockings and then stood. Holding my skirts aloft, I stepped in the stream.

It was delicious.

I closed my eyes, letting the rushing water and playful breeze carry me away, far from missing Thomas, far from the dark tower of Markham Hall.

A stick snapped. My eyes flew open and I saw Mr. Markham watching me from the bank of the stream. He said nothing, eyes flicking from my bare feet under the clear water to my face, his posture anything but casual or accessible.

Should I say something? Was I doing something wrong? Maybe he felt possessive of his property and disapproved of the liberties I was taking with it?

He stepped forward to the bank. "Are you a naiad?"

I could not tell if he was sarcastic or playful. I should tread carefully here, be wary of the conversational missteps that Thomas had complained I was so prone to. But it was difficult to be wary in the perfection of the stream and the flapping greenery, with the bluebells swaying in the warm breeze. Instead of answering, I reached down and splashed him.

The water splattered the front of his waistcoat. He glanced down at the drops rolling off the silk of his vest, watching as they rolled off and hit the ground. He looked back up, his expression inscrutable—though there was a tightening around his mouth and along his jaw—and then without another word, he turned and walked away.

I watched him leave, feeling regret nip at me.

Why did I do that?

It was just that his face had been so serious, and I had wanted him to smile, I had wanted him to join me, and now I had driven him away with my ungovernable behavior.

Suddenly, the rushing water became unbearable. I went to the bank and shoved my wet feet back in my boots, my skirts dripping the whole way back to the tower.

When I came downstairs for dinner, I once again found myself alone for dinner.

"Mr. Markham preferred to dine alone tonight," Mrs. Brightmore told me, with entirely too much pleasure. "He was quite in an ill humor when he returned from his business in town."

Ill humor that was my fault.

I was served soup that was too cold and rolls that were too hard, and no beverage other than water was offered, and by the time the miserable and lonely repast had ended, even the bleakness of my room seemed like a welcome alternative. I decided to stop by the library on my way up, peruse the books for a selection or two to keep me company tonight. Surely, I would not be called on to spend the evening with Mr. Markham, and even more certainly, I wouldn't feel welcome in any other part of the house if I was by myself.

This morning, I had felt the faintest glimmer of optimism. I'd felt it possible that I could belong here and call this dark and ancient manor my home. But as the sun went down and the house became once again dim and quiet, all those feelings vanished. Instead, I found myself looking over my shoulder as I walked to the library, feeling as if someone were watching me, although every time I turned, I found nothing more than shadowed paintings and faded tapestries in my company.

I hadn't thought to fetch my lamp from upstairs or ask for a candle, and so the murk of the library was pierced only by the last glancing rays of the setting sun as they spilled in through the windows. I ran my fingers along the cracked leather and cloth spines, only able to make out the ghosts of the letters in the gloom. I paused when I got to the end of the shelf. There in a small glass case was a miniature, cunningly done, of a young woman with bright yellow hair and blue eyes. At first glance, I thought it might be Violet, but then I saw the name at the bottom: *Arabella Markham*. The first wife, the one who had died so young.

Every room in this house seemed to remind the living of the dead. Portraits of dead wives and ancestors, tapestries of battles and assassinations.

I shivered and straightened, realizing that the chill night air had slowly overtaken the room. I selected a book at random and hurried to my room, where I stoked the fire that had been lit—perhaps thanks to my new friend Gareth—and changed into my nightclothes. I tucked myself in bed with a candle and wondered if this would be every night at Markham Hall. If I would never again drink port with my benefactor or feel his fingers on my skin. All because of one playful infelicity.

Several hours later, I woke with a start. There must have been a noise, yet when I strained my hearing, the house seemed altogether still and silent. But not sleeping. Markham Hall didn't seem the type of abode to give the impression of repose or sleep. There was something watchful and alert even in its stillness, as if the stones themselves were too charged with history and drama and death to be at rest.

I struggled to light my lamp in the dark and then slid my feet into my slippers. I wasn't sure if I was planning on investigating or simply escaping my room—something about the sliver of moon and the twinkling stars called to my soul, promising safety and relief as soon as the walls of the house were no longer around me.

I encountered nothing conscious or moving as I went to the door, nothing save for a cat that padded past me without any indication of interest in my person or my movements. I pushed open the heavy door as quietly as I could and stepped outside, into the chilly air. Almost at once, I felt like I could breathe again, think again. The forest creaked and swayed in the wind, but the noise did not frighten me. It was quite comforting after the hush of the house.

I walked the perimeter of the courtyard, again and again, until I felt the telltale pull of exhaustion within me, and then I went back inside the house, temporarily blinded by the contrast of my lamp in the pitch-black foyer.

I stumbled into someone; strong arms steadied me, hands encircling my upper arms.

"Miss Leavold," a voice said. I knew without raising my lamp that it was Mr. Markham.

Should I apologize? Explain myself? Or would such gestures further alienate him?

"I was walking outside," I explained.

"I see that."

Just then, my lamp guttered, the oil insufficient to sustain the flame. I felt the lamp taken from my hand and set on a nearby table. The expanded circumference of the failing light allowed flickering glimpses of Mr. Markham's face, of the dark stubble and even darker eyelashes, of the square jaw and the somewhat wide mouth.

"Are you so wild that you cannot even sleep in a bed at night?" There was a lift to his lips as he said it.

"It depends on the bed," I answered, meaning to jest, and too late realizing the implications my reply made.

His eyes glittered and then the lamp went out, plunging us into darkness. For a moment, there was only breathing and no movement, and then, ever so softly, I felt a thumb brush across my cheek. My breath caught and my stomach flipped, and nothing that I had ever felt before matched this terrified delight that I felt right now.

The thumb moved across my jaw and then finally to my lips, pressing against them, making urges and imaginings swirl through me. All I could think of was how Mr. Markham's stubble would feel against my cheek or even against my bare stomach...

I shuddered and without thinking, parted my lips and bit his thumb.

He may have flinched, but I could neither see nor feel it in the dark.

"Go to bed," he said, his voice cold and hard. "Leave me."

I hurried up the stairs, quickly shutting myself in my room, my breath still coming in erratic rhythms. But it wasn't fear or regret that tugged at me. It was the memory of Mr. Markham's thumb on my lips, of his eyes glittering in the dark.

Chapter Four

Sleep was elusive the remainder of the night. Why had Mr. Markham touched me? And why had I bitten him when he did? I knew only that it had been instinct, spurred on by the tightening knot in my belly, a knot he himself had tied by touching me so unexpectedly, so gently. I'd been around men so rarely at home—Thomas and our old gardener being the exception—but even I knew that the behaviors I exhibited around Mr. Markham were far from customary. Presumptuous. Shocking, even.

But though I'd never been touched by man in any meaningful way, my body knew exactly how to react when my new benefactor touched me.

Before the sun had completely risen, I dressed, arranged my hair and went downstairs to the kitchens. I wanted to avoid another lonely breakfast accompanied only by congealed food and Mrs. Brightmore's scowls. If I went directly to the kitchens and took my food there, they'd see that I didn't expect anybody to bow and scrape before me. At home, I'd eaten either outside or in the library anyway—just as well, since by the end, only the pottering old gardener and his daughter had remained on to help. There would have been no elaborate, multi-course dinners even if I had wanted them.

The smell of warm bread greeted me. I ducked under the low threshold, the stone walls and floor cool and damp despite the heat coming from the ovens and the fireplace. An older woman sat chopping vegetables for the day's meals and a young child—seven or eight perhaps—tended the large ovens and the central fire, where turkeys and Cornish hens were being roasted to provide cold meat for the day's dinner.

"Hello," I said tentatively. "I thought I'd spare Mrs. Brightmore the trouble of serving me breakfast and come and get it myself. I was thinking about taking a walk; would it be all right if I simply took some bread and some cheese?"

The old cook creaked to her feet. She came up to me and examined me, but without any cruelty or scorn as Mrs. Brightmore had done, only with curiosity. I dredged up her name from an overheard conversation. Mrs. Wispel.

"You do look a bit like her," the cook said at last.

"Like who?" And then I realized. *Violet.* She could only mean Violet.

"Different coloring, of course. You look a bit gypsy, if you don't mind me saying, but you could just as easily claim Italian. But the face—I can see something of her there." She nodded. "But you've got a good heart, I can see it in your eyes. A good open heart. Not like her."

"I'm sure Violet—"

Her expression tightened. "We don't speak the names of the dead here. Too close to the churchyard. It will waken them, make them

32

restless."

This must be some sort of Northern tradition we didn't have in the south. "Sorry," I said. "I mean, I'm sure *she* didn't mean to give the impression of having a bad heart. I remember her as very energetic and happy."

"She only lived for pleasure," the cook said, crooking a finger at me, as if Violet's Epicureanism had been my fault. "And that always turns a heart rotten, like fruit left too long in the sun."

She trundled over to the table and gestured to the boy. He pulled a fresh loaf of bread from the oven while she unwrapped a wedge of cheese. "Mind you, she was right unhappy in the end. Like you, sneaking down for her meals so she wouldn't have to eat with her husband. Claiming she was too hungry to wait for regular mealtimes. And the rows they'd have; I'd hear her cries coming from his bedroom at night, shattering glass from the parlor...it weren't no surprise when the constable had to ask Mr. Markham all those questions."

"There was an investigation into her death?" This was the first I'd heard of it. I'd been under the assumption that everybody had accepted the tragic nature of her accident.

The cook nodded, slicing off a thick hunk of cheese and setting it next to the bread. "The saddle had been ruined in some way—cut partially, so that it might tear, especially if the rider was riding at a gallop or at a canter, like she often did. Of course, the constable didn't have much leeway—it's difficult to accuse a man like Mr. Markham, you see. In the end, they called it an accident. But the village knows what really happened. Mr. Markham's been such a cold, unknowable person, ever since he was a young man. Cold and peculiar. When his father died, he was only seventeen, and rather than take on his duties and settle down as he should, he went off to Europe. And the stories that came back..."

I accepted the bundle of bread and cheese; at the last moment, she reached over and placed a shiny red apple on top. "What kind of stories?" I asked.

"Not the kind a young lady should hear." But she glanced over at the child. I made a note that she might speak more if she were only in adult company. Extrapolating from our conversation now, I surmised that she wasn't the kind to hesitate to share her opinions.

"You speak rather freely of your employer," I remarked.

She eyed me, again without animosity. "I've worked in this house since I was younger than that one." She used the cheese knife to point at the child. "Any loyalty I had died with the old missus and master. And the young master knows that, just as he knows he won't find a better cook anywhere in Yorkshire."

"Sounds like a tenable arrangement," I said. "Thank you for the food."

She snorted. "It was nothing. I'm always happy to feed you, but don't let that Brightmore woman drive you away from the table. You're a lady and you live here now. She doesn't know her place. Thinks just because Mr. Markham brought her in as a maid from another big house and raised her up to the level of housekeeper that she's better than service and better than all of us here. I wouldn't be surprised if she cherished the hope that the master will fall in love with her, like in those awful novels everybody seems to read these days."

I was on the stairs when the cook called after me once more.

"Be careful, Miss Leavold."

On my walk? "What do you mean?"

"Markham Hall already has two dead young women to its name," she said.

"Accidental deaths," I pointed out.

But she simply shrugged and turned back to her chopping, not bothering to elaborate or explain, and I was left unsettled.

It was past dawn outside, yet the sun stayed behind the clouds; fog filled the grounds and the space between the trees, making the world silver and strange. I walked down the path, thinking to eat by the stream again, unnerved at how quickly the world behind me was swallowed up by the mist. It swirled around my boots and skirts, clung damply to my hair and dress, and it was only the lonely sound of the stream that gave me any sense of distance at all.

I continued, walking further than I had yesterday, stopping finally at a place where the stream widened into a glassy and shallow pool. I ate my still warm bread and cheese, thinking of all the cook had told me. Did she really suspect Mr. Markham of murder? Or did she only say such a thing because it dovetailed nicely with her opinions of his behavior as a younger man? Had the constable really investigated him for Violet's death?

And what about Violet? I could imagine her being unhappy in a marriage. She had been friendly—*too* friendly—wanting to talk to anyone who would listen to her giggle and flirt...which had been everyone who met her. Shut up in this dark house, so far away from London and Brighton and her other favorite places, with someone as remote and mercurial as her husband, I could easily see her suffocating. And Violet had never kept quiet about a single iota of unhappiness in her life. Every imagined slight, every small boredom, became a pain too intolerable to be endured and everybody within earshot heard about it.

Yes, yes. An unhappy Violet would fight, would cry and yell and hurl glasses.

But that she would avoid her husband, sneak into the kitchens...that seemed so unlike her.

Could she have been genuinely afraid of her own husband? Afraid for her own life?

The water rippled, churning into one end of the pool and then spilling out the other. On impulse, even though it was not warm by any means, I began to take off my boots and stockings, wanting to be in the water. With a glance around the fog-draped banks to make sure I was still alone, I also took off my dress, corset and petticoat so that my long chemise was all that remained.

I stepped in the water, cool but pleasant, feeling the smooth river rocks beneath my feet. My arms and chest erupted in goose bumps and everything seemed to tighten and contract in the cool water. I waded in until I reached the deepest spot and the water lapped against my navel. Without giving myself too much time to think, I dropped underneath the surface and swam in a small tight circle, loving the feeling of the cool water on my scalp, loving the way it filled every crease and fold of my body. It was freedom. From gravity, from noise, from breathing itself.

I emerged, gasping for air and sweeping my hair back from my face, and that's when I saw him: Mr. Markham, once again watching me as I played in the water.

This time, I did nothing. I neither spoke nor splashed, and I waited as silently as he did, watching fog wisp across the pool, my heart pounding madly in my chest.

Without a word, he stepped into the stream, boots and breeches and all, coming towards me with long, assured strides, even in the water. The mist between us danced and eddied until it vanished, only to reassemble in his wake. We were now together in the center of the pool, completely surrounded by fog. It felt as if we were in our own small world, as if we'd been transported to Avalon and we were the only two living mortals there.

I expected him to speak and to address last

night when I had bitten him, or before, when I'd splashed him with water. I expected him to chide me once more for being wild.

But normal rules didn't apply here, not on otherworldly mornings in the middle of a forest.

He reached one arm out, and I thought he meant to take my hand, but instead, it snaked around my waist, pulling me tight against him. I could feel the warmth of him through his clothes, warmth that reminded me of how chilled I was. He pressed his forehead against mine, his eyes closed.

"You were supposed to be a charity case," he said. "Or a houseguest. Or family. I can't remember any more."

"I am happy to be anything you need," I said. "I am grateful—"

He continued on as if I hadn't spoke. "I got the letter from Solicitor Wickes the day after she died. He'd addressed it to her, of course, not knowing she was dead. And the thing was that I felt by helping you, maybe I'd be helping myself. Erasing a black mark from my record. Although the Lord knows there are too many marks to ever hope to be clear of them all."

"How can I help you then?" I said. His face, so close to mine, touching mine, made it impossible to breathe or even think normally. "Please tell me."

Our noses touched and my breath hitched. That knot deep within me was burning and twisting, and I wanted to press closer to him, to touch him and slide my fingers against his wet skin.

He pulled back. "You can't help me," he said. "You can't be what I need. Nobody can. I've learned that the hard way."

He glanced down, and to my surprise, he groaned. I looked down too, only now realizing that my swim had made my chemise completely transparent and that my erect nipples were dark and hard under the thin fabric. For the first time, I was completely aware of how violently inappropriate this all was—me standing nearly naked, allowing myself to be embraced by a man who'd only been widowed a month. Every aspect of this violated those rules my parents and Thomas had attempted to ingrain within me.

I should feel ashamed. I should feel compromised.

But I did not. I only felt that tightness low in my belly, those urges, and when he slowly bent his head and took my cold nipple in his mouth, my cry of pleasure was unsullied by any other feeling. He sucked me through the thin cotton of the chemise, and it was so warm, the only warm thing touching my body. He nibbled and teased and pulled with a fervor that was arousing in and of itself, as if this small act were the only thing he wanted to do, not just now, but for the rest of his life.

My other nipple tightened, and my core muscles clenched, and all those dirty words that Violet had taught me as a girl flashed through my mind.

Cock.

Cunt.

Fuck.

Abruptly, he stopped and straightened. The absence of his mouth on my breast was akin to physical pain; the delicate area between my legs throbbed with need.

"Please," I whispered. "More."

His eyes were once again shuttered, once again remote. Without another word, he climbed out of the pool and left, the fog swallowing him up before he'd even reached the path.

Chapter Five

"Mr. Markham has sent me to request that you dine with him." Mrs. Brightmore's voice left no doubt as to how she felt about this, even through the thick wood of my door, and I wondered if the cook was right, if she fancied herself in love and waiting tragically for a man who could never marry her. I wondered if he had ever touched his housekeeper like he had touched me. Certainly not recently, but perhaps when she was younger? She had high cheekbones and thick hair, large eyes and a delicate jawline. It was easy to see where she had once been beautiful, where hard work and loneliness and resentment had eaten away at a fine face. The thought made me surprisingly jealous, even though I knew such things were not uncommon, servants being with masters.

You have no claim on him. You barely know him.

But still.

I started to change into a nicer dress, my stomach somersaulting as I contemplated going downstairs. I'd spent the day in my room, pacing, unable to stop fixating on the memory of Mr. Markham's dark head at my breast. I could recall every minute detail of the moment: the soft abrasion of the fabric against my skin, the heat of his mouth, the movements of his tongue. And I found that as I thought, my hands drifted to my breasts, trying to recreate the sensations, the tight web of desire forming at the base of my spine once more.

I paused my dressing. I sat on the bed and spread my legs, ignoring the faint voices telling me that such a thing was not done, too shocking for a girl of good birth to even think about. I pulled the gown up to my waist and let my hand drift towards my center. Where was this loudly clamoring need located? That knot of desire? I felt as if I could unravel it, as if I should, because seeing Mr. Markham with it throbbing inside of me would surely compromise my ability to be collected and calm.

My hands found my folds, which were slick, and then I found the small bundle of nerves at the top. This too Violet had told me about, although I'd never tried touching it as she had once gigglingly suggested.

I rubbed experimentally and a jolt of pleasure shot straight through me. I rubbed again, unconsciously pressing against myself, rocking my hips back and forth, wondering what it would look like to see Mr. Markham's hands down there, stroking and sinking into me—

A knock at the door.

"Miss Leavold?"

I slid off the bed, cheeks flaming. It was Mr. Markham. Thank God he hadn't let himself in unannounced.

"Yes?" I managed.

"I just wanted to make sure Mrs. Brightmore

passed along my express wish that you be in the dining room with me tonight." His voice left no room for argument. Even if I hadn't already agreed, I would feel compelled to acquiesce now.

"Yes, of course. I'll be there in only a minute."

His footsteps echoed down the hall, and I hurriedly dressed, hoping nothing about my face or behavior would betray what I'd just done.

Dinner was almost entirely silent, save for the clanking and clinking of dishes and silverware. I could think of nothing to say to him that I could say with Gareth waiting on us, and whenever I looked at him to try and find an innocent topic of conversation, my gaze zeroed in on his mouth, sensual and curved as he ate and drank, and on his hands, which I had just imagined doing such wicked things.

"Miss Leavold, will you join me in the library?"

"Yes," I murmured, feeling Gareth's eyes on my back as I pushed my chair back and left the dining room.

A warm fire had been lit and so had the heavy chandelier, so the room seemed less shadowed than it had last night.

"Port, Miss Leavold?"

"Yes, please."

He poured two small glasses and handed mine to me, our fingers touching briefly as he did. A small shudder of delight raced through me. He noticed.

He walked over to the fire, and I arranged

myself on a nearby sofa, wondering what safe subject I could broach; I found myself both terrified that he would talk about this morning and terrified that he wouldn't.

"I am so sorry that I didn't get to see Violet again. Before she died." The moment the words left me, I noticed that Mr. Markham's mouth had parted, as if he were about to speak himself. But at my statement, his lips pressed together again and he gave a nod.

"Yes. Yes, I imagine you are."

I was reminded of the cook's suspicious rumblings and I wanted to ask about the screaming and the shattered glass. About the investigation into her death. But even I knew better—even I could see how rude such a line of questioning would be.

His face was turned to the fire. "You are the first good thing to happen in this house since she died. Or since we married."

I waited for him to continue.

He didn't.

Instead, he went over the library door and turned the lock, coming back to the sofa. He sat, his leg pressed against mine, and I imagined I could feel how muscular it was, even through the layers and layers of clothing that separated us.

His posture was casual as he drank his port, and I followed his example, setting my glass down on a nearby table when I'd finished. I felt warmer, happier somehow. More relaxed. More daring. Perhaps I could talk to him about what happened today. I turned toward him.

"Mr. Markham, about today…"

"Yes?" His tone betrayed nothing but polite interest. I could have been asking him about the weather or the latest levy on carriage wheels.

I continued, fortified by the wine. "I don't want you to take an unfavorable impression of me from it."

He laughed. "I intrude upon you in a private moment, take advantage of you, and you don't want *me* to think badly of *you*?"

"I guess I hadn't thought of it in those terms," I said, frowning.

His laughter faded away, replaced by a serious expression. "I've been thinking of it all day." His fingers trailed against my hand and up my sleeve, until they came to rest against the bodice of my dress. "What are you?" he asked. "Some kind of spirit sent to tempt me?"

"I could ask you the same question." And I couldn't help myself. I had to touch him. I ran my fingers along the stubble on his jaw, marveling at the roughness of it, how scratchy it was and yet how soft the skin underneath. My hand dropped to his thigh, where I felt how right I had been—his legs were muscular and firm.

He jumped off the couch, running a hand through his hair. "Do you have any idea what you are doing to me?" he demanded.

My heart jumped. He was just as affected by me as I was by him, and that realization thrilled me beyond measure. "Sir—"

"*I told you not to call me that.*"

"I am sorry for causing you distress—"

"Distress," he stated flatly. "Yes, you are causing me immense distress." He came to a stop in front of me. "Have you ever even kissed a man?"

I felt a little insulted. Despite what had happened here at Markham Hall, despite my admittedly untraditional upbringing, I had never done anything of the sort. I may have been wild, but I wasn't loose. "Of course not," I said. I'd meant to sound indignant that he'd even asked, but my voice betrayed something else: longing.

"You see? You are completely virginal, though Lord knows those lips and eyes don't look the part." He shook his head, as if to clear it. "You have all of these firsts—kisses and caresses and more—left in front of you. You are completely fresh to the world of grown men and women."

He took hold of my hands and helped me stand to my feet. "I think it's best if we keep our distance from one another," he said. My whole body wilted in disappointment. I wanted nothing less.

"Why?"

He pressed his forehead against mine just as he had this morning. "Do you remember me saying that I had become a creature of needs after Violet's death? I wasn't exaggerating and I wasn't joking. I'm accustomed to getting what I want. And I want you."

"What's wrong with that?" I managed to ask.

"Why can't we want one another?"

"You don't understand what I mean. When I say that I want you, I don't mean your company or your conversation. I don't want to pine over you and write you poetry. I mean," he pronounced carefully, "that I want to bend you over this sofa and slide inside of you. I mean that I want to pin you to the ground and watch you squirm as I drive into you over and over again. I mean that I want to spend my evenings watching your pretty little head bob up and down on my cock."

He took my hand and pressed it against the front of his breeches. There indeed was the object of his words, hard, so very hard, and thicker than I ever imagined. The knot inside of me threatened to snap. I wanted all of those things too, I realized, too aroused to feel embarrassed or shameful. I wanted him inside of me and I wanted to feel his mouth on me once more...

"You see now," he said, lifting his head and looking me in the eyes, "why you must stay away from me. You don't want to be the kind of woman who lets a man fuck her just so she'll have a roof over her head."

It took only a second for the meaning of his words to sink in, what he was implying about me and my sense of dignity...not to mention what he was revealing about his own concept of hospitality. My blood turned hot, scorching my own veins, ire pounding through me.

I slapped his face as hard as I could.

"I'm not a prostitute, and I'm more than capable of surviving on my own if I have to," I said.

He turned his face slowly back to me, a handprint blooming on his cheek, each finger clearly delineated in bright red. I wanted to hit him again and again until he apologized, but as I raised my hand, he caught my wrist. We wrestled for a moment, his arms coming around my waist, and before I knew it, I kneeling on the floor, both of my arms pinned behind my back. He knelt in front of me.

My breath came quickly and adrenaline pumped through me, but it wasn't fear I felt but a feverish rush instead.

"Oh, my little wildcat." His voice was rougher than normal. "You give me no choice. I have to take this one thing from you. Just this once."

He pressed his lips against mine. They were soft, oh so soft, and warm, and then he gently parted my lips with his own, and slid his tongue inside my mouth.

I wanted to pull him closer, wrap my arms around him and never let go, but they were still pinned behind my back, and his grip tightened as he deepened the kiss, as if he knew exactly what I wanted to do.

Our tongues met, silky and flickering, and I moaned into his mouth, the sensation so delicious, so perfect.

After what felt like several thousand heartbeats later, he broke his lips away from mine but remained close, so that I felt the breath of his words.

"I am going to try my hardest not to ruin you," he said. "I am going to try my hardest not to touch you again, after tonight."

He released my wrists, but I didn't move them, almost missing the restraint. His hand slid up my skirts and under my chemise.

"Are you scared, Miss Leavold?"

In response, I parted my knees as far apart as I could, my body overriding my brain to give him access to whatever he wanted, because it was what I wanted too.

If I looked down, I could see him straining against his pants, but other than his thick erection, he gave no outward sign of his lust. He seemed perfectly calm and in control as his fingertips traced spirals up to my center, his eyes fixed to my face, his chest swelling with deep, even breaths. The moment he made contact with my clitoris, I inhaled fiercely, shuddering. His fingers moved down.

"So wet," he murmured. "How can you be so wet from a single kiss?"

"It's you," I managed to gasp out. "You are the one doing this to me."

His arm wrapped around my waist and yanked, so that I slid on the wood floor a few inches, spreading my knees even farther apart. One arm held me tight, while the other was under my skirts, and God, *the things he was doing there*.

"I am doing this so you can see why I need to stay away from you," he said. One finger slowly

49

pushed inside of me and everything within me shuddered and clenched and I let out a single, desperate, "*Oh.*"

"You're so tight now," he said, his lips now near my ear. "You have a tight little cunt and the man you marry will want it to stay that way. It's so perfect and so wet, and he will want to be the first to feel it around his cock." The finger moved deeper and deeper, until he reached a spot that made me writhe and push against that hand; all the while, he held me with his other arm, kept me pressed against him.

"And with your perfect cunt around me all the time, with those perfect breasts and that plump mouth, if I don't make myself stay away, then I can't answer to what will happen."

"What will happen?" I whispered, needing to hear more, his words making everything in me tighten around his expert finger, making my body quiver and tense all around a central point deep inside of me.

His grin was wicked. "Then I *will* bend you over that sofa. I'll watch you wrap your lips around me and suck until I'm satisfied, and then I'll fuck your pussy until I spill inside of you. And once we start, there will be no stopping. I'll have you in every room of this house, on every surface. I'll make you climax as often as it suits me, even if it's several times an hour for an entire night. I'll make you thrash underneath me and beg, and maybe if you're good, I'll let you ride me and use me until you're too limp to keep yourself upright any longer.

"And I'm sorry. I lied earlier...because I am taking one more first from you," he said, and then he plunged two fingers inside of me, his thumb pressing once more against my clit in small, fast circles.

The quivering in my core was almost too much to bear. I grabbed on to Mr. Markham's suit jacket, feeling almost panicked.

"Mr. Markham, please..."

"Please what, wildcat?"

"I...I...don't know." The tightening felt as if it would split me in half if I let it, as if it would unravel my entire being. How could I possibly survive something so strong, so elemental, a tidal wave threatening to surge and crash on top of me and—

He pressed his lips once more against mine and the wave crashed, my body shook, the muscles in my pelvis and inner thighs and belly convulsed and released and convulsed again. I thought I would die, the waves went on so long, radiating to every part of my being, all centered on his hand under my skirts.

I came to, fumbling my way out of an unimaginable glow, to find him supporting almost all of my weight. With no visible exertion, he lifted me easily into his arms, walked to the library door, unlocked it, and carried me to my room.

He laid me in bed and I stared up at him, sharply handsome even in the dark, unable to speak or think or feel beyond the small waves of pleasure that still pulsed through me.

"Lock your door at night, wildcat."

"Why?"

White teeth flashed. A grin.

"Because of me."

Chapter Six

I slept better that night than I had slept since Thomas died—or possibly even since my parents died. When I woke, the sun was already streaming full in the window, signaling that mid-morning was not far off. I closed my eyes once more, pretending it was firelight that glowed through my eyelids, pretending that someone's arms were around me, that expert fingers were caressing me and coaxing me to that state of exultation once more.

I wondered why I didn't feel guilty or regretful that I had allowed such liberties last night. *I should feel guilty.* I hadn't been in a church since my parents died—with the sole exception of Thomas's funeral—but I did remember the clergyman constantly referencing The Unchaste Woman as the source of society's ills. In our library at home, there had been many tracts in the same vein, as if Thomas wanted to make up for his frequent absences and excesses by at least ensuring I had the right sort of literature around.

But what Mr. Markham had done to me last night hadn't felt wrong. Nothing had felt more right—as if he and he alone were created to touch my body. I decided to ignore the clergyman and the dusty tracts. What did it matter, really? Mr. Markham spoke of a future husband, but surely a smart man like him could see that a husband was unlikely for a girl as poor and unconnected as I was.

No, in all likelihood, I would spend the remainder of my days alone, at the mercy of others, and it wouldn't matter how pure I'd been.

Knowing that Mrs. Brightmore would judge me for lying in, I decided to make every effort to avoid her today. After dressing and putting up my hair, I settled on a walk to Stokeleigh to post a letter to Solicitor Wickes thanking him for all of his help in securing me a place to stay.

My plan was ruined when I encountered Mrs. Brightmore on the staircase, me with my letter in hand and her with a bucket of steaming water.

"Pardon."

"Out of my way," she snapped.

I'd only been here a few days, but I'd never seen her attend to any of the drudgery work herself. "Do you need any help?" I asked tentatively.

"You'd probably just muck everything up," she said and pushed past me, slopping hot water onto my dress.

I came the rest of the way down the stairs, hot with anger, and was met by Gareth carrying a cord of firewood. He stopped, but behind him I saw a few other servants moving in and out of rooms, carrying rugs to be beaten and mattresses to be aired.

"Everything all right?" he asked.

"I'm perfectly fine," I said.

He raised an eyebrow, and I realized that my fists were clenched, crumpling my letter in the process. I took a deep breath and relaxed my fingers. "What's all the bustle about?" I asked him.

"Ah, that." He shifted the firewood so that he could brush some of the blond hair out of his eyes. "Mr. Markham has invited a party of his acquaintances to come stay a while. Several men and women. Markham Hall hasn't had visitors since I can remember—Mr. Markham prefers to go off to see his friends—so there is quite a lot of work to be done."

Visitors? I wondered why and why now, so soon after Violet's death. And then I felt a sharp pang of disappointment. Despite what Mr. Markham had said about not touching me again, I still wanted to see him and talk to him. I wanted him all to myself. I didn't want to share his company with a party of his friends and risk him ignoring me. I knew I was being unreasonable, that I was only the orphaned girl kept out of some distant sense of duty and charity, and that I'd only known him for a few days, but I didn't care. I would tear this house apart, stone by stone, if it meant we could share another night like last night. And besides, I didn't like large crowds of refined people. Making strained polite conversation and pretending to laugh at stale witticisms exhausted me. I'd much rather hide in the library or escape outdoors.

"Are you going into town?" Gareth asked, nodding at my letter.

"Yes," I said, forcing myself back into the present. "To the post office."

"Could I escort you? Mrs. Brightmore wants me to requisition more help for the house."

I agreed, and after he finished with the firewood, we started off together, down the winding sun-dappled lane to Stokeleigh. Birds sang and animals chittered as we walked; summer felt as if it was poised to explode into heat and growth any second. The more we walked and the further away from Markham Hall we got, the less my thoughts centered on last night and the more they alighted on more troubling matters.

"Gareth," I asked after we'd been walking in companionable silence for several minutes. "The cook said something to me yesterday that I've been thinking over. She said that the constable had investigated Violet's death as if it had been a murder. Is that true?"

"She told you that, did she?" Gareth scratched his face. The gesture was oddly endearing, as if he were a young man just growing his first beard. "You shouldn't listen to old Wispel. She likes nothing more than to tell stories."

"But is it true? She'd said that the saddle cinches had been cut."

He rubbed at his face again, clearly uncomfortable. "Her death was investigated," he admitted. "But they found no cause to suspect Mr. Markham. They ruled it an accident."

"No cause? Or they didn't want to accuse a man as powerful as Mr. Markham?"

Gareth stopped, his blue eyes pained in the happy light of the forest lane. "I know she's your cousin and so you feel the need to know the truth and that's why you are asking. So please believe me when I say, from the bottom of my heart, that no one in the world would ever lift a hand to hurt her."

"But that's not entirely true either, is it? Mrs. Wispel said Mr. Markham and Violet fought— violently even."

He hesitated. "It's true that they did not get along well after they married. But if you could have seen him while they courted—he was a man entranced. He took me along with him to London— usually he hires a valet from whichever city he's staying in—but I think this time he wasn't planning on staying long. Just a day or two. And then he met her at a ball. He came back to the hotel that night, vowing to win her hand. And he did. It took months, but he did."

"How romantic."

"I suppose. Mr. Markham began bringing me more frequently on those trips and I got to see their courtship firsthand." He paused again, as if unsure how to phrase his words. "Your cousin was very pretty and very well-liked, but there were rumors…"

I nodded. "I knew Violet's temperament. It doesn't shock me. Continue."

"Rumors that she was more than flirtatious. *Carnal* rumors." There was a color to his cheeks now, although his expression wasn't suggestive of bashful innocence. Growing up with older brother had taught me what young men liked to joke about, and I could easily picture Gareth listening and sharing those same rumors. The coloring came from guilt, I decided, from indulging in the salacious tales surrounding the newly dead.

"I'm sure there was nothing to them, of course," he continued, "but there were some who said she would not be a proper wife. This didn't bother Mr. Markham at all—he seemed almost excited by her reputation, as if it presented a challenge. And there were many who thought that if any man could bring her to heel, it would be Mr. Markham."

"So what changed after they married?"

He hesitated. "I don't know. It started slowly at first—not talking during dinner, spending afternoons apart, that sort of thing. All she wanted to do was go back to her old life in London; I think she thought that marriage would be the same as being single, except with more money and with a large house to her name."

That sounded like Violet. "And what do you think Mr. Markham thought marriage would be like?"

"He had been married before, but only for a month. Who knows what he expected from Mrs. Markham?"

"And then the fights grew worse?"

"Loud. Messy. They'd say things to one another that would make you cringe to hear them. She'd pound her fists against his chest and lob whatever was near at him, and he wouldn't hit her back, but he'd issue such cruel remarks that he might as well have struck her." His voice went low and strange. "He didn't understand her. He didn't deserve her. She was caged in that house, she was lonely and deprived, and he wanted to keep her isolated and all to himself. And now she'll never leave Yorkshire."

His words made the summer air heavy and we walked the rest of the way in silence. We arrived in Stokeleigh ten minutes later, the small village I had been unable to admire on my ride through a few days ago. Charming and small, its three principal streets lined with snug cottages and one cluster of ancient timber and plaster shops, it was a cheerful place, seeming in its bright industry to be miles away from the brooding manor house rather than a short walk.

Gareth directed me to the post office, touched his cap and went off to complete his business. Bells tolled from the tiny stone church as I walked into the post office. After paying my penny, I went back outside, meaning to wait for Gareth at the edge of the village, but I was approached straight off by a prim-looking girl who seemed about my age. Her navy poplin, trimmed with lace and set off by a large brooch, spoke of modesty and wealth. Her wedding ring glinted in the sun.

"Hello," she said, and somehow in one word, she managed to pack in both condescension and obsequiousness. She held out her hand. "I'm Mrs. Harold, the *rector's* wife." The emphasis on *rector* made it clear exactly where she thought her place in the community was—at the very top.

I shook her hand, trying to discreetly search the street for any sign of Gareth. "Ivy Leavold," I said, warily.

"Oh yes, we know who you are." At the *we*, she turned and looked knowingly at three women behind her whom I hadn't noticed before. They looked as young and stiff and self-assured as Mrs. Harold did. Discomfort prickled at my neck and shoulders; I was always at sea with groups of people, especially well-dressed, judgmental groups of people. "*You* are the new girl who's come stay at Markham Hall."

She seemed awfully gossipy for being married to a man of the cloth. The wheels turned and clicked in my mind, and I realized she was going to pump me for information, search me for all the juicy morsels of news she could carry and then disseminate around the community. I looked around for Gareth again.

"Is it *true* that you are Violet Markham's cousin?" she asked.

"Yes." I supplied nothing further.

"And that you had *nowhere* to go after your brother died?"

I bit off the irritated remark that floated to mind. "Yes," I said instead.

"And that they had to sell your family's house to pay off your brother's *debts*?"

That stung. Of course, as advertised as the auction had been, it would be easily discoverable knowledge for anyone who wanted to know—but still. The thought of my snug home, nestled so close to the sea cliffs, now lived in by strangers...

"Yes," I finally answered. "Yes, it was sold."

She gave the others a satisfied look, as if pleased to prove that this piece of information was, in fact, correct. "You poor thing, you must be so grieved. If you *ever* need someone to talk to, I am here. It is my job, you know, to help tend my husband's flock."

"Thank you for your offer," I said. "It is so very kind."

"Miss Leavold!"

Gareth. At last.

He hurried over, a sunny smile on his face, and the other women pretended not to notice him, stealing brief glances out from under their eyelashes. He was below them, a servant, and so to be ignored, but his good looks made it all but impossible not to notice him.

"Mrs. Harold," he greeted. "Having a nice day?"

"Nice enough," she said, her tone dismissive. But I saw that she noticed him too, although her look was wary rather than flirtatious.

"It was very pleasant to meet you all." I said turned away before more invitations could be offered. Gareth touched his hat to the ladies, and then followed me up the street.

His smile faded the further we got from Stokeleigh. "I would avoid that Mrs. Harold," he said. "Her husband, the new rector, is quite nice. Very young, very cheerful. But she grew up here, and she's known to be a gossip. I wouldn't trust a word she says, no matter how earnest it sounds coming out of her mouth."

"I gathered that."

"She's worse than Wispel even. Her father has made a small fortune in negotiating land rights for the train companies. She seems to think all that money has made her better than everybody else."

I detected a trace of bitterness. "Have you known her long?" I asked.

"Yes." He turned his face away. "And we know each other still. A bit."

We walked in silence the remainder of the way, and I contemplated Mrs. Harold. As the town busybody, she would know all about Violet's death and investigation, and she wouldn't hesitate to talk about it. Part of me felt certain that it was foolish to keep asking about it—if the law had been satisfied, surely I must be. And Violet and I had hardly been the best of friends. And Mr. Markham couldn't be a murderer. The thought of someone so cultured and moneyed resorting to something so barbaric was unthinkable. And yet, there was a darkness in him. Hadn't I seen it—thrilled at it even—when he had told me all of those things on his library floor?

Perhaps I would be paying Mrs. Harold a visit soon.

Chapter Seven

The next evening, there was a rap at my door, followed immediately by an attempt to turn the knob, which was stymied by the lock. The door rattled in its jamb for a moment before I heard Mr. Markham's voice. "Miss Leavold. Let me in, please."

I went to the door but did not open it. "Is it wise for me to open it to you?"

A short laugh. "I assure you, I am quite tame at the moment."

I unlocked the door then stepped back. He opened it and strode in, looking around the room. "It is very gloomy in here," he remarked.

"I think you would struggle to find a room in this house that is not."

"And does that bother you?" he asked. "Coming from the sunny seaside as you did?"

"It does not," I answered truthfully. "In fact, I very much like it here."

He sat in an armchair by the window. "That is unexpected. Violet hated it here. I think she hated this house more than she hated anything in her life."

"I am not Violet," I said.

He looked at me. "No. No you are not."

As he looked at me his fingers flexed and curled over and over again on the arm of the chair, and I wondered if they were remembering being inside me and remembering the soft sensation of quivering flesh, how they had brought me to such intense ecstasy.

"Pleasant memories?" he asked, and I realized he had caught me staring at his hand.

"I thought you were going to stay away from me," I said instead of answering, hoping the warmth on my face wasn't too obvious.

He grinned. "I was. I am. But I remembered in all the bustle of getting the house ready for the guests that you might not have everything you need."

"I'm sure—"

"Let me see your dresses," he interrupted. "All of them."

My flush turned from one of desire to one of embarrassment. Though I knew that Mr. Markham had exchanged letters with Wickes and knew the precise details of my impoverishment, something about laying out my three outdated dresses was especially humiliating.

Seeming to understand the source of my hesitation, he said, "This is not to shame you. But in a few days, we will have many guests. There will be dinners and picnics and long evenings in the parlor—maybe even some dancing. You are under my care, and your material goods reflect on me. If we need to order you new dresses, then that's what shall happen."

There seemed no point to arguing the matter. Either he would see them now or he would see them when I wore them after the guests arrived. I brought out the three dresses—one nice black silk that I had worn to Thomas's funeral, the faded green lawn, and a calico that I'd inherited from the curate's sister back home. These, in addition to the dress I wore, were the only things I owned.

Mr. Markham surveyed the clothes. "Could your brother truly not afford to keep you better outfitted than this?"

As always, I felt the need to defend Thomas. "He was often traveling on business, and I didn't like to bother him with such petty requests."

"You mean he was away gambling and carousing." Mr. Markham didn't wait for me to respond. "I know all about your brother's habits. Needless to say, if you had been in my care, I would have never so neglected your company or your upkeep. But regardless, you are in my care now, and I will see this rectified. Expect the seamstress tomorrow."

He stood and I moved in front of him before he could walk to the door. "Mr. Markham. You have already been beyond generous by inviting me to stay with you. You know I can't importune you any further, as I don't foresee any way that I could ever hope to pay you back. If my wardrobe is an object of ridicule among your guests, then that is my problem, not yours. I assure you, I'm used to being poor."

"It is my problem," he said, "because you are under my roof and I have accepted responsibility for you." He rubbed at his forehead, more agitated than he'd let on. "Under what domain will you allow me to contribute? We are family, are we not, through marriage? Or perhaps simply as your benefactor? I don't care what you have to tell yourself to accept them, but you are wearing the dresses I order for you, if I have to come up here and lace you into them myself."

"I'd like to see you try," I shot back.

"Oh, wouldn't you like that, wildcat? If I had to come up here every night and strip you down?" His hands found my arms. "If I had to wrestle you until you were subdued and willing?"

My breath was coming faster now, imagining how such a scenario would end—with bites and moans and sweat. "Who's to say I wouldn't win? Perhaps you'd be the one subdued, Mr. Markham."

"We'll never find out unless we try," he said, a touch mischievously.

There was a moment that consisted only of us breathing, looking at one another, both thinking the same wicked thoughts.

Then he removed his hands from my arms. "Will it make you feel better," he asked with a sigh, "to know that the expense of the dresses will barely be noticeable in my ledger? I kept Violet clothed in all the latest and finest while we were engaged— several new purchases a month—and even that was easily affordable to me. As a widowed man without children, I have much more money than I know what to do with. So please. It will cost nothing to me and it will make me immensely happy to help you."

I could not even conceive of a wealth so vast that the purchase of several dresses a month would seem like a drop in the ocean. I saw his point, and yet... "It is only that I don't like to be indebted to people," I said. "And I am already so much in your debt."

His green eyes were dark, almost black, in the lamplight. "Then we will have to work out a way for you to pay me back."

I liked that idea very much.

The seamstress indeed came the next day, all the way from Scarborough. She took my measurements, warning me that only two or three dresses would be done by the time the guests arrived, but that she would rush the rest of the order and hopefully get more to me next week.

"And exactly how many dresses are in the order?"

"Twenty-three," she said without batting an eye.

I was staggered. That was double the number of dresses I'd owned in my entire life.

"Mr. Markham has picked the patterns and fabrics himself," she continued, wrapping a tape around my waist and then scribbling on a scrap of paper. "You will be quite pleased." If the seamstress knew of my impoverished state, she didn't say anything, but when I shifted my feet to hide the holes in my stockings, she did mention that Mr. Markham had also thoughtfully ordered me new undergarments as well.

Later that morning, I accompanied Gareth once more to town, and when word got around the house that I had some experience gardening, I was pressed into service gathering fresh flowers and greenery to fill the guest rooms. Mr. Markham was absent— *he's gone away for business*, Mrs. Brightmore had informed me curtly when I'd asked—and I felt as if the day were meaningless without him there, as if the possibility of talking to him was the only thing that kept me grounded in reality. Instead, I spent my spare time roaming the woods, swimming and daydreaming. Everywhere I walked, every place I swam, I harboured the secret wish that he would appear out of thin air as he had before.

He didn't.

The next morning came, dawning warm and golden. I realized I'd been in the house almost a week. Such a paltry amount of time, and yet what had happened in that week. Meeting Mr. Markham, learning more about Violet, being *touched* in such new ways...

I decided to go swimming again, partly to cool off and partly because I hoped that by recreating the other morning, I could somehow conjure Mr. Markham from thin air. It didn't work, but I felt refreshed and content as I emerged from the pool. The morning sun had burned off the fog and the day promised to be hot, although a line of dark clouds in the distance augured rain later. I gathered my things and went back up to the house, pausing in the gardens behind it to gaze at the blooming flowers and beating butterflies.

"Miss Leavold."

I turned, my heart pounding, both exhilarated and slightly terrified that my wish had been fulfilled. "I was just admiring your beautiful gardens."

"I know. I was just admiring the woman admiring my gardens." His eyes took in my wet hair, my rumpled dress, my lack of corset. "You went swimming again."

I raised my chin, not intending on apologizing. Surely it harmed nothing to swim in such a remote pool? And surely my time and activity wasn't beholden to anything here? It hadn't been at home.

"Let me give you a tour," he said, changing the subject and his tone abruptly. He clasped his hands behind his back and started walking, and I followed, unable to keep myself from noticing the way his tailored jacket highlighted his wide shoulders and narrow hips.

We walked through a low maze, past a large fountain and into a small side lawn set with a temple folly, all surrounded by a verdant circle of trees. The rainclouds had encroached faster than I had earlier guessed; a dark line of shadow bisected the lawn as the clouds rolled overhead.

"Are you going to say anything?" I asked.

He looked at me in surprise. "What do you mean?"

"I believe it is traditional when giving a tour to speak a little on the subject. You might, perhaps, tell me when this folly was built or which one of your ancestors built it?"

"Are you really so fascinated with this ruin?"

No. I just want to have you all to myself. I want you to touch me again.

"Why wouldn't I be?"

He sighed. "Fine. Let's examine it closer."

The temple was circular, green-roofed, and without walls, completely open to the world. Unlike most follies, this one had a circle of low stone benches inside, making it into a pretty retreat. I ran past Mr. Markham to mount the steps to the temple and clamber on to them, for no other reason than that I wanted to.

He watched me with some amusement. "You are something apart, Miss Leavold."

I jumped down, landing as lightly as a cat. "So you tell me."

The wind picked up for a moment, tossing the leafy branches into a rustling susurrus, and then the rain began, a slow, steady drizzle.

"We should get back to the house," I suggested, gathering my skirts to make a run for it.

"Nonsense. We'll get soaked."

"So?"

The rain intensified, turning from a light and clinging mist into an opaque curtain of silver. Mr. Markham took my hand and led me into the center of the small temple, where the roof protected us from the worst of the downpour, although gusts of wind still whipped droplets onto our damp clothes and hair.

"We'll wait it out," he said firmly. "It won't last long."

I looked longingly out—running through a deluge like that looked like an enlivening adventure—but then when I looked back at Mr. Markham, my heart stuttered and I realized that there was no place I would rather be. Especially when he was looking at me the way he was now, with darkly green eyes and a mouth that looked nothing so much as hungry.

"Sit, Miss Leavold."

"What?"

"Sit down."

I sat, not knowing why and also not knowing why I found it so easy to obey when I was so unused to obeying the whims of anyone other than myself. He knelt in front of my knees.

"You have made a mistake," he said. "You've let yourself be alone with me."

"How do you know that wasn't my plan all along? You were the one who promised not to touch me. I never promised not to touch you." And I ran my thumb across his lower lip. It was soft and slightly wet from the rain.

He bit it and the sensation went straight to my core. I took in a breath.

His hands slid up my ankles, past my low boots, and up my calves and thighs. I'd planned on a quick swim, so I hadn't worn anything underneath my dress. He discovered this when he reached my upper thighs.

Now it was his turn to draw in a breath. "Miss Leavold," he said huskily. "You have been very bad today, haven't you?" He rucked up my skirt, drawing it up to my hips. "Let's see exactly how bad you've been."

The skirt was now bunched up around my waist and my pussy was exposed to the open air.

"It was just so I could go swimming," I explained, a little breathlessly. He looked ravenous.

"Was it? And were you not hoping you would also run into me?" He ran a finger down my folds and I shuddered.

"I was hoping that." I couldn't lie with his fingers on me.

"Hoping what?"

"To find you."

"And?" A hand reached up to caress my breast. I moaned.

"And that you would touch me again," I whispered.

"I want to, wildcat. I do. But I have promised you that I wouldn't."

"Please," I said breathlessly. "Just this once. I'll do anything…"

He continued running his fingertips along the most sensitive places, stopping now and again to swirl gentle circles on my clitoris. The rain made a solid sheet of privacy around us, but at that point, I didn't care. The entire kitchen staff could have gathered around to watch Mr. Markham pleasure me, and I would have still begged him to keep going.

"Anything?"

"Yes."

"I will make a note of that." And then he did something unexpected—he bent his head down and licked along my seam. The feeling was so soft and sent such an electric jolt through me that I gasped. He impatiently pushed my legs further apart and put his tongue to me again, this time concentrating on my clitoris, alternating between pressure and light flicking motions that stirred me into a frenzy.

"You taste so good," he said in that growling voice of his. "I could do this all day. Would you like me to?"

I nodded. I wanted his mouth on me always. And yet, as I looked down and saw the stiff outline pressing against the front of his pants, I thought I could also happily trade places and spend my days with my mouth on him. The mere thought made me almost wild with desire. My hips bucked, and I ran my fingers through his hair, tugging as he sucked and nibbled and licked.

"How does it feel, Ivy?" he asked.

"Wonderful," I managed.

He slid a finger inside of me and I couldn't control the way I pulled at his hair. If it hurt, he made no mention, but the corners of his mouth turned up, as if my wildness pleased him.

"I'm the first to taste you," he said. "The first to taste this perfect cunt. And it is so perfect, Ivy. So damn perfect. If I had my way, I would fuck it right now with the whole world able to watch."

"Please." I could see us in my mind now, see his hard cock pressing into me, and nothing sounded better. "I want you inside of me."

"You don't know what you're saying," he said roughly and then he bent his head down again. He sucked and teased at my clitoris while his finger slid in and out, finding just the right spot inside of me to make my toes curl and my core clench. I looked down, seeing the top of his head between my thighs, seeing my skirt around my waist like a whore, and then it was over. Just as quickly as it had built, the tension in my body imploded, starting as a series of contractions at my center and radiating out to every digit, every muscle.

Mr. Markham withdrew his finger, pulled back as if to examine his work, and, after giving my pussy one last look, stood up. I stayed where I was, legs still spread, secret parts of me still exposed, and my eyes fixed on his erection.

I reached for it and Mr. Markham let me, closing his eyes as I ran my fingers along it. With a sigh, his eyes sprang open. "Kneel," he said. I scrambled to my knees, at this point eager to do anything he asked. Eager for more of this type of play. My body burned for it.

He sat down and began unbuttoning his trousers. "Look at me," he said.

I couldn't tear my eyes away from his hands, his long fingers slowly but deliberately working the buttons through the buttonholes. "Look at my *face*,

Miss Leavold."

I did. He drew out his cock and my eyes drifted back down. "At my face," he reminded me, not so gently.

I looked into his eyes, trying to focus on the way the rain made them shimmer and dance, and not on the fact that his hand was moving slowly, lazily, up and down his rigid length. I couldn't help it—my eyes dropped again, drinking in the length and thickness of him, and then his other hand was in my hair, jerking my head back.

His eyes searched mine, all while his hand moved faster. "You tasted so good," he said, his voice betraying no pleasure or exertion as he worked himself. "So sweet. I could stay with my face between your legs all day. Would you like that?"

I couldn't nod with his hand pulling so tightly at my hair, so I said, "Yes."

"You are making it very difficult to be a civilized man," he said.

"I don't want you to be civilized," I whispered. I meant it.

He groaned, letting go of my hair and letting go of himself. "This is wrong. I'm taking advantage of you."

How could I make him see that he wasn't? That I *wanted* this? I reached out a hand and circled him with my fingers. He made to brush me away, but I used my other hand to stop him. "Just this once," I said. "This is twice that you've given me something, and I don't like feeling as if I owe you."

He looked at me, his jaw set, and then he wrapped his hand around mine and guided me, squeezing my fingers and moving them up and down, up and down, until I could see the pulse pounding in his throat and the muscles tensing in his thighs.

He pulled a handkerchief out of his vest pocket. "Look at my face, wildcat." I did, amazed at how calm and in control he seemed. "Move your hand."

As soon as I did, he wrapped his own around his cock, the silk handkerchief in between his hand and his skin, and gave a soft breath. He kept his eyes pinned to mine as he brought himself to climax with two precise strokes. I had never seen anything so contradictorily erotic—there he was in the open, bringing himself to orgasm as I watched, yet his self-possession and coolness as he did was just as arousing.

He tucked the handkerchief back in his vest, buttoned his fly and then stood, offering me a hand. "It appears the rain has let up. Shall we brave going back to the house?"

I stared at him. His posture and his tone gave no indication that he had just ejaculated into a square of silk not thirty seconds ago. Something panged in my chest, a worm of fear that he would forget about this, forget about *me*, and pretend this hadn't happened.

But what could I do? I was completely dependent on his goodwill for everything. I needed Mr. Markham to survive. More than that—

something deep within me—my soul or my self or my true mind—needed Mr. Markham's presence and affection to thrive.   I craved his presence, his company, even if it meant that at this moment, I had to bite back the need to somehow claim him or to mark this moment as special.   Instead, I took his hand and let him pull me to my feet. He got to one knee and before I could ask him what he was doing, he was gently rearranging my skirt so that the dress fell evenly to the ground. He stood once more and then we walked in the now temperate drizzle back to the house.

Chapter Eight

It was the day that the guests were to arrive. A man from town delivered my dresses a few hours after breakfast, and when I pulled them out of their boxes, I was entranced by the brilliantly colored silks and satins. I'd never cared much for clothes—when I had so few, such an obsession seemed pointless—but now I felt as if I could die happy. I'd never owned anything as fine in my life as these.

The boxes also contained new corsets, stockings and other underthings. I stroked the silk stockings, wondering how soft they would feel against my skin. I carefully arranged the dresses in the wardrobe's tray drawers, and then spent the rest of the day gathering more flowers for the parlour and dining room.

Around mid-afternoon, the courtyard erupted in a song of wheels and horseshoes, loud shouts and calls exchanged between the parties in the different coaches. I had been placing more flowers in the library when I heard them; I went to the window to watch the guests arrive.

Women arrayed in flowing skirts and bunched bustles spilled out of the coaches, and the accompanying gentlemen rode up alongside them, dismounting their horses easily and helping the women alight onto the flagged courtyard, their number impossible to count once the maids and valets emerged into the fray. They were all young, all happy, all noisy. All unbelievably good-looking. My heart sank as I watched them crowd into the front door. I wondered how many of the women were single and if any of them were hoping to exploit this opportunity to snare the wealthy new widower who lived here. And surely, around so much beauty and wealth, Mr. Markham wouldn't spare a thought for me?

You're being stupid, I told myself. But still, I made my way upstairs with haste in order to avoid the inevitable flood of guests and trunks in the hallway.

Dinner was set for eight, and so at seven-thirty, I found myself in front of my vanity, completely dressed and with nothing to do but wait for thirty minutes. The dress I'd chosen was a deep crimson, a silk that looked apple red in places and almost black in others. Even though I had my doubts about wearing such a daring color, the dress was the only one with a neckline that didn't make me blush to look at. This dress still exposed the very tops of my breasts but nothing more, and it was cut in quite a trendy fashion, with off-the-shoulder sleeves, a long waist and an elegantly draped skirt that allowed my new slippers to peek out from underneath. I put my hair up as elaborately as I knew how, thanks to the sister of the curate's passed-off fashion magazines, and finished the look with a black ribbon tied around my neck.

I didn't look bad, I thought, standing up to

admire myself further. The crimson and black went well with my Iberian coloring, and the dress made the most of my curves and height.

The doorknob rattled, as if someone were trying to open it. My breath seemed to rattle inside me in response, my whole body suddenly alert and excited.

I hurried to unlock the door and open it, and there he was, leaning against the doorjamb, looking every part the wealthy landowner with his black tails and trousers. He had shaved, with the effect he looked ten years younger, and his hair was trimmed and swept back from his face. I bit my lip, thinking of touching his now-soft face, of mussing that carefully placed hair. Of the way his smooth cheeks would feel as they brushed against my thighs.

He froze at the sight of me, then, taking a quick look around the hallway to make sure no one would see, he stepped inside and closed the door. And locked it.

"I see you got your new clothes," he said, now letting his eyes trace every curve and tuck of the dress. His gaze lingered on the choker. "Might I say, they suit you quite well."

"Thank you," I said.

He seemed as if he were about to continue, but then he caught sight of my face and paused. "What's wrong, Miss Leavold?"

Was I that transparent? Probably—I had so little experience lying. As the only inhabitant of my house, it had been unnecessary growing up. "Why did you invite your friends to stay?"

He raised an eyebrow. "Do you mean so soon after Violet's death or so soon after your arrival?"

"I don't know. Both."

"I told you that I didn't feel like this house would be at all fun for a young woman, as cut off and quiet as it is. I made that mistake with Violet, and I won't make it with you."

"I told you that I didn't care," I said. "I like this house, I like the quiet and the solitude. I'm not like Violet!" I don't know why I felt so vehement about this, only that I felt as if sometimes he only thought of Violet when he looked at me, of her flaws and weaknesses.

"I *know*," he said patiently. "But this house can drive even the most forbearing person mad if they're left alone in it too long—believe me, it's why I've left so many times."

He seemed sincere enough, but I still couldn't shake the beginnings of resentment for his guests, jealousy of the undoubtedly interesting women who would crowd the dinner table tonight.

"And," he said after a pause, "I invited them because I needed something to distract me from you."

"You didn't have to do that," I said. "I could have stayed out of your way…"

He picked up a feather that had fallen from a new hairpiece. "But I think we've established that I cannot stay away from you—" He shrugged. "I'm hoping that a house full of people will keep you safe, for a while at least."

"What if I don't want to be kept safe?"

He used the feather to trace a line from my earlobe to my jaw, down to my neck and to the tops of my breasts. "Then I would say that you are in a lot of danger, indeed."

Mr. Markham escorted me downstairs to supper, all traces of pique and desire vanishing under a face of impermeable impassivity. We met the other guests outside the dining room, and then Mr. Markham led the way, with me on his arm. I flushed at this unexpected honor, although as the resident female in the house, it shouldn't have been unexpected. The others whispered to each other as they followed us and took their seats, the men waiting until all the ladies had settled before sitting themselves.

Servants hired from town came in, wearing full livery, and began serving steaming bowls of soup and pouring glasses of wine. While they worked, I made note of the thirteen guests. There were five men—all handsome and all in their mid-thirties and younger, and eight women, again, all young, all vibrant. Not a single wedding ring could be glimpsed among them, and I wondered at the possibility of having such a diverse party where not one member was married. Where had Mr. Markham met these people?

One woman in particular caught my eye. She had bright red hair and a smattering of freckles across her nose. Vibrant blue eyes and a pink pout of a mouth. Her pert bosom highlighted a slender waist and hips, her bare arms showed a lean and sculpted strength, and everything about her suggested a sort of schoolgirl sensuality, a cape of innocence drawn over extensive knowledge.

"So you are the mysterious cousin Julian wrote about," she said. It took me a moment to realize that Julian must be Mr. Markham; I hadn't known his first name until now.

"Ivy Leavold," I supplied.

"Mary Margaret O'Flaherty, and don't ever call me that, call me Molly." She looked at Mr. Markham. "Jules, you never mentioned that she was so pretty. That will make it a lot harder."

"Miss O'Flaherty," Mr. Markham said in a warning voice.

"Make what a lot harder?" I inquired.

Molly leaned forward, the lace trim around her bodice casting intricate shadows on her creamy breasts. "Why, Julian here put us all under strict instructions not to include you in our fun."

He sighed.

"Fine," she amended. "It was phrased more like: *on pain of death, you are not allowed to corrupt her.*"

"Corrupt me?" I thought he had brought them here to save me *from* corruption? And what kind of people were these, anyway, that could be capable of such a thing?

"I think," Molly lowered her voice to a confidential whisper, "that our Julian here would like to corrupt you all by himself."

"This is hardly dinnertime chat," he said. "And besides, you'll scare off Miss Leavold before she's even had the chance to truly make your acquaintance."

"If she's going to be living here, I imagine she'll want to know what kind of people you consort with, Jules."

"Where did you meet?" I asked, hoping to bring the conversation back to territory I understood.

Molly's mouth curved. "In Amsterdam, years ago. You should have seen him then, Miss Leavold, fresh from the death of his first wife, quite lost and ragged looking. A man running from his past, like Byron's Giaour, returning to his old haunts from before his wedding. Of course, he was irresistible to all the women there. He could have had his pick of some of the finest ladies Europe had to offer, but our Julian isn't the easily-married kind. He amused himself in other ways."

Her provoking tone and his non-response made it clear what kind of amusements he'd found, and instead of being shocked or upset, I only found myself worrying that he'd amused himself with Molly O'Flaherty. What if, upon her staying here, they resumed that relationship? Jealousy flared up at the thought, and with it came a concurrent pain, sharp and unexpected. And foolish. Julian Markham wasn't mine to be jealous of, for one thing, and that he might be attracted to the woman across from me was only understandable.

I felt something brush my leg, and I realized

Mr. Markham was giving it a reassuring squeeze through my dress, under the table and out of sight. I looked up, our eyes met, and there was that lust again, the lust he'd so skillfully hidden. Something soft and thin was placed in my hand—the feather from upstairs. I twirled it under the tablecloth as the conversation continued around us, Molly's keen eyes on me the entire time.

I learned the names of the guests. Adella, Charlotte, Ettie, Helene, Mercy, Rhoda, and Zona, along with Molly, comprised the women, and Gideon, Hugh, Ned, Owen, and Silas made up the male portion of the party. Although they were all English, save for Hugh and Adella, who were French, they were part of the same extended circle of friends that Mr. Markham had collected while abroad. And in the two hours that our meal lasted, I could detect something different and exotic about them—something of the amusements that Molly had so teasingly mentioned.

They frequently touched each other and lingering kisses were not uncommon. Stories were referenced in low voices, followed by giggles and gestures that made their subject matter quite possible to discern. Most unusually, they didn't seem to be coupled in exclusive pairs. Blown kisses and caresses were shared by all, even by those of the same gender, so that by the time dinner was finished, I could have been forgiven for thinking that perhaps Europe was the haven of sin that the curate of my childhood parish had led me to believe.

But the old curate would have been horrified to learn that, instead of shock, I felt only curiosity. What would it be like to kiss and touch someone so openly? To press my lips against Molly's plump, pink ones? Or to once again kiss Mr. Markham? I desperately wanted to try, but instead I kept hold of the feather like it was a promise, keeping it in my fist until it was time for the ladies to rise and go to the parlour.

When we entered, I made sure to take a low seat in back, out of the way and partially out of sight, hidden beyond an end table laden with flowers. I still felt unease around all these strangers, and that unease tripled as soon as I left Mr. Markham behind. I looked longingly at the window, which showed a welcoming velvet night outside.

"I'm already bored," Helene declared, tossing herself onto the sofa. "Why must the men stay and talk forever when we are all ready to play?"

"We could find that cute servant boy," Ettie suggested. "That would make the men wish they'd hurried up."

"What shall we play?" Rhoda asked. She was the tallest of the women, with pale blond hair and strong features that made her look like a goddess from Norse myth. Zona, her fraternal twin, was much the same, although with hair more golden than white.

I knew it was typical for card games or parlour games to be played after dinner, so I wasn't surprised when Molly declared that we would play charades once the men joined us.

"Although," she said pointedly, "we will have to be more subdued than normal."

This elicited a chorus of groans from the women, along with some pouting, which only served to make them look lovelier.

"But why?" Helene asked.

Molly threw a meaningful glance in my direction, and I wished I'd found an even more out of the way spot to sit. The others turned towards me, curious and irritated.

"Oh," Ettie said. "That's right. You're Julian's new pet."

"I'm a relative of the late Mrs. Markham's," I said, hearing how defensive I sounded.

"Ettie," Molly scolded, "you've quite put her out. Look at the poor girl—she looks like a wild animal backed into a corner."

Truly, that's how I felt. Though the women were nothing but intrigued—if condescendingly so—my body thrummed with energy and adrenaline, as if it thought I were under physical attack. The fantasy of running out of the room became blindingly sharp in my mind, and I even shifted my feet under my dress to stand.

"Well, I don't see why we need to act any differently just for *her*," Helene said.

"It's not for her, it's for Julian," Rhoda said. She offered me a kind smile. I decided that I liked her.

Molly walked over. "Girls, this isn't way to treat our new acquaintance." She took my hands and pulled me to my feet. "I promise we aren't normally this cheerless about new friends. We will have so much fun during our visit, and I think you will have fun with us. Can I tell you a secret?"

I wanted to shake my head. I wanted to pull my hands away and run out of this room and out of this house. But something about Molly was magnetic. Cutting and mendacious, but magnetic.

I nodded.

She put her mouth against my ear, her breath hot on my skin. "I don't think it's fair for Julian to keep you all to himself and then not play with you, like a trinket in a glass case. Perhaps you and I can change his mind?" And then she nipped at my earlobe, taking it in her teeth and flicking her tongue over the sensitive skin there. As soon as it started, it finished, and she was moving back across the room, throwing me a daring glance over her shoulder.

I put my hand to my ear, not sure how I felt about her proposition or her unexpected touch.

The door to the parlour opened and the men entered, led by Silas, who seemed to be the leader of the party. His pale skin made his dark brown hair and blue eyes stark, mesmerizing, but his engaging laugh and easy smile kept his beauty human and approachable. All eyes followed him as he walked in and gracefully folded himself into a seat, already smiling and joking as he sat.

"You finished your conversation early," Molly

noted to Mr. Markham.

"I didn't want to leave poor Miss Leavold too long in the viper's nest," he said. His tone was light, but there was a warning in his words.

"Oh, we've been behaving ourselves, Jules."

"Mary O'Flaherty behaving herself. Shall I alert the newspapers?"

Without waiting to see her reaction, Mr. Markham turned and walked to the back of the parlour, back to me. As he approached, my vantage point from the stool gave me an entirely different view of his body, namely of how tightly his trousers clung to his muscled thighs and how this highlighted an even more interesting part of his body. He'd removed his dinner jacket, and so now I could see that lean waist and how it led up to that chest and those strong arms that had so effortlessly carried me to my room a few nights ago.

He sat next to me. "Are you comfortable? Entertained?" he asked.

"Of course she is," Silas laughed. "She's with us. And we will show her such entertainment that she'll be spoiled for amusement with anyone else."

"Charades," Molly announced. "We shall play charades."

Silas leapt to his feet. "I claim Miss Leavold for my team."

Mr. Markham's posture stiffened. "And I assume I'm on your team as well?"

"Don't be a fool, Julian, where's the fun in that? No, you and Molly must be together, as you always are."

There was a possessiveness in Mr. Markham's touch when he helped me stand so I could walk across the room, but he didn't argue. And it wasn't a hardship on my part—as nervous as I felt around these people and at the prospect of playing a game I'd only played once or twice before—Silas's infectious energy was impossible to be immune to. When I reached him, he took my hand, kissed it and swept into a bow. "My lady." He tugged me very close and leaned in conspiratorially. "We must defeat Julian's team. He always wins and it's really quite unfair to the rest of us."

This made me smile.

"She smiled!" Silas exclaimed. "And here we all thought that happy faculty had been stripped from her." His eyes stayed on my face. "And now that I have seen it, I have decided that my life's work is to make you smile as often as possible, for a smile as luminous as that can only be the handiwork of God himself, and are we not all called to do the Lord's work?"

His words were in jest, but his thumb rubbed across the back of my hand as he said them, and there was an intensity in his gaze that made heat spread across my cheeks and down my stomach.

"Silas," Ned said. "You'll frighten the girl off before we even start."

"We can't have that now, can we?" My hand was squeezed once more, then dropped.

Even from across the room, I could feel Mr.

Markham's eyes burning into my back.

Chapter Nine

Mercifully, the game began before Silas could flirt with me any more. Various scenarios and words were written onto pieces of paper and then tousled together in a large bowl. Silas volunteered himself as the first from our team to play. He read the paper, a smile twitching on his lips, and then slid it into his pocket. I let the others shout out their guesses as he began to walk unsteadily around, shoulders hunched and face scowled, as if on a ship in rough weather. Then he mimed a bird flying above, then a gun, then the bird's death.

I opened my mouth, then closed it as the others kept calling out guesses around me. Silas saw me and nodded encouragingly.

"Rime of the Ancient Mariner," I said.

Silas pulled out the slip of paper for the other team to verify and then bowed, winking at me as he slid back into his seat. One tally mark for us.

I watched Mr. Markham as his team whispered about who should go first—Molly, it was decided—and then I watched as she gave him a playful squeeze on his thigh as she stood. His face remained still, giving no acknowledgement of her touch, but envy flared through me, hot and quick. I looked down at my hands as she drew her slip of paper, trying to regulate the sudden wash of resentment I felt towards Molly.

Up in front, Molly made no reaction as she

read her challenge, only gave the others a slight nod to show that she was ready to begin. Her eyes fluttered closed and her breathing picked up, speeding into quick pants and sudden, sharp intakes of air, as if her breathing was interrupted by some other sensation that only she could feel. Her head lolled back and her hand reached up to fan her face.

"This is too easy," Silas said disgustedly.

"*Shh!*" came from the opposing team.

She continued fanning her face as her fingers traced a trail from her neck to her breasts. She let out a low moan. In front of me, I saw Ned shift in his chair and cross his legs.

"The dog days of summer," Mr. Markham called out.

The charade abruptly stopped and Molly grinned. "A tally for us, I think. And Silas, we don't all have minds as depraved as yours."

"You've never complained about my depravity before, Mary Margaret, and I know you won't be complaining tonight."

There were laughs, but there were also knowing looks, and Silas's was the most knowing of all. Once again, I felt at sea, out of my depth with these sophisticated people. In a way, I wanted to be like them—familiar with pleasure to the point of dismissiveness. But in another, much stronger way, I still wanted to be outside, away from their sidelong looks and veiled references that I only barely understood.

The game continued in the same vein for

another hour—each charade, though perfectly innocent on paper, inevitably turned into something with sexual overtones. As the game wore on, the suggestion of sex became less of a suggestion. Ned pulled Hugh up and kissed him long on the lips to demonstrate the story of Jonathan and David. Mercy unlaced her dress to give herself the bedraggled appearance of a shipwreck survivor. On and on it went, my face flushing warmer and warmer, and not from embarrassment, until Molly and Silas claimed exhaustion and stopped the game while it was tied. Laughter and conversation bubbled up and drinks were called for; I used the friendly chaos as a screen to escape quietly from the room.

The hallway was much cooler than the parlour, and I continued down it until I reached the low door that led out to the gardens, grateful to feel the open air on my face and to be on my own once again.

"Am I interrupting you?" Mr. Markham asked from behind me.

"Not at all." I slowed my steps so that he could catch up, and together we walked in the moonlight, the light breeze and chirruping of insects the only noise aside from our footsteps on the path.

"Did you enjoy yourself this evening?" he asked.

"Your friends are more worldly than me. I'm afraid I'm a social liability." I meant it lightly, but he stopped and gazed at me with fierceness that surprised me.

"You are not at all a liability. Quite the

opposite. They are all very taken with you."

"I hope I've made a good impression. Silas is very friendly."

This, apparently, was not at all what Mr. Markham wanted to hear. "Silas is dangerous."

"He seems the very spirit of good humour."

"I meant dangerous to young women and their virtue."

"As dangerous as you?" I asked.

His eyes glittered in the dark—more silver than green in the moonlight. "I am much, much more dangerous." He stepped closer, so that the rustling silk of my gown brushed against his legs. "And now that I've felt what it's like inside you, now that I've tasted you," he said quietly, "I'm hungrier for you now more than ever."

Our faces were very close now, and I vividly recalled the warmth of his lips, the soft dancing of his tongue. On impulse, I pressed the palm of my hand against the front of his breeches, feeling the thick hardness underneath.

He sucked in a breath.

I moved my hand up and down, rubbing him through the expensive fabric, and his eyes slowly closed.

"The others called me your pet," I whispered to him. "Would you like me to be?"

He gently pulled my hand away. "That's what I'm trying to save you from."

And then he bowed and walked away, the gravel crunching under his boots as he went.

I didn't return to the others. Instead—new dress be damned—I left the grounds and entered the forest, luminously lit by the full moon and the glut of stars overhead. I paced and walked and fretted, imagining conversations and kisses, creating scenarios that ended in passionate embraces. It wasn't until I found myself at the pool where Mr. Markham had so unexpectedly claimed my breasts that I came to a decision, a decision that had been brewing the entire week but that I hadn't yet articulated to myself.

I wanted Mr. Markham. I wanted him in all the carnal ways that he wanted me, and I didn't give a damn about the consequences. I had no money and no connections and my claim to the title of gentleman's daughter was now completely laughable. I would never make a good marriage, if I ever made one at all. Perhaps being a mistress was the best I could hope for. Certainly, being one to Mr. Markham would be no hardship. He was handsome and darkly unpredictable, intelligent and generous with his pleasure. He haunted my thoughts day and night, every hour, every minute, and I thirsted for his company like a forest for rain. I was obsessed, I knew, obsessed in a way that spoke almost more of love than of lust.

Mr. Markham had told me that he was a man of needs. But wasn't I also a woman of needs? Roaming wildly, drinking whenever I liked, swimming and running and reading late into the night? For the last seven years, I'd followed my impulses wherever they led me, and it was too late to stop now.

No, I wanted him and I wanted him tonight. I would find him and tell him, and if he insisted on restraining himself, well, then I would do everything in my power to shatter that restraint.

I picked up my skirts and hurried back to the house. I must have been gone longer than I'd thought because the windows on the ground floor were quite dark, though the upstairs windows held flickering lights, indicating that the guests had retired to their rooms. I entered the house as silently as ghost, not wanting to disturb people preparing for sleep, and crept through the rooms to make my way to the staircase, wondering how I would find Mr. Markham now. I didn't even know where he kept his rooms, much less if he would be in them at the moment.

But my search ended when I heard the unmistakable sound of kissing coming from the drawing room. I froze, not wanting to be caught, listening to the heavy breaths, the soft noise of lips meeting and parting.

"Oh, Jules. You need to be put out of your misery." It was Molly O'Flaherty's voice.

"Please," a voice groaned. A rough voice. Mr. Markham.

There was more rustling. "Are you sure?" Molly said, her voice teasing. "Are you sure that's what you want?"

I didn't stay to hear what he said in response. I hurried upstairs as quietly as I could, tears burning in my eyes as I shut the door and climbed fully clothed into bed.

I barely slept. What sleep I managed to steal consisted of vivid dreams of Mr. Markham and Molly together, twining and writhing together, and whenever I awoke from such a vision, a twisting pain in my chest made it impossible to fall back asleep.

My jealousy had been warranted. There was something between Molly and Mr. Markham, not just sex, but a history of sex. Of course, Mr. Markham had been with other women—nothing he or his friends had said would have led me to believe otherwise—but that he could be so physical with me, claim to want me so badly, and then share his body with Molly so soon afterwards—it stung. No, it was worse than stinging, it was a wound, packed with the venom of jealousy and insecurity and doubt.

By dawn, I was out of the house, possessed of a basket of food from Wispel's kitchen. I was determined not to torment myself by watching Markham and Molly together at the breakfast table, and I was determined not to mope indoors. I walked further afield than I ever had, past the boundaries of Stokeleigh and into the slowly tumbling fields beyond the forest. By noon, I found the exercise had numbed me somewhat, anesthetizing my mind from the memory of Mr. Markham's rough voice, the way he had begged *please.*

I had chosen a narrow lane to take back to the house, debating about staying outside for the remainder of the day, when I had to stop to make way for a small phaeton that was passing by. But the phaeton halted and none other than the rector's wife, the gossiping Mrs. Harold, held the reins. It seemed precisely my luck.

"Oh my, Miss Leavold! How can you be out and about in all this *heat*?"

I searched for a diplomatic answer, fumbling, my interior pain making normal discourse all but impossible. "I find walking to be quite enjoyable."

"Are you walking back to Markham Hall now? *Please*, let me give you a ride!" She scooted over and tucked her skirts back, and feeling as if I had no choice, I climbed in beside her.

"Thank you," I said.

"It's nothing at all. Is that a new dress, Miss Leavold? You are done up *quite* well today."

Something told me she was mentally comparing today's frock to the dress I'd been wearing when we first met in the village. Comparing, and mentally ticking away each yard of silk and lace. She had to know that Mr. Markham had furnished me with something like this; there was no way I could have afforded it myself. But I didn't care that Mrs. Harold would inform the village of this sartorial charity and I didn't care what they would think. Only my own opinion mattered.

And Mr. Markham's.

Mrs. Harold took my silence for confirmation. "Now, please," she said, snapping the reins. "You must tell me all about the party up at the hall. We saw those coaches rolling through the village yesterday, and the rumor is that Mr. Markham is hosting almost *twenty-five* guests."

"Thirteen," I corrected.

Her eyes glinted at this fact. "And do you know all of their names?"

I allowed that I did.

"And where are they all from?"

I told her that they had come from London and had been friend's of Mr. Markham's when he had traveled abroad, but that I had went to bed early last night, and so my knowledge was still very limited. She nodded at this, filing away the little tidbits I'd given her, no doubt already expanding and speculating on them, readying them to be shared amongst her flock of village women.

"Is it true that Mary O'Flaherty is there?"

"You know her?"

"Of course not. She's *Irish*, you know, by way of Liverpool. Do I look like someone who knows a lot of Irishwomen?" She didn't give me time to answer, not that I would have volunteered one anyway. "But everyone knows *about* her. Her father owned one of the largest shipping companies in Liverpool. He died a few years ago, and instead of passing on the business to a male relative, she decided run it *herself*." She shook her head, as if Molly had decided to parade naked through the streets instead of follow in her father's footsteps.

"So she's wealthy," I said. Another thread of pain laced itself in my heart. Lovely and rich. I would never be able to compete with that.

Mrs. Harold didn't notice my change in tone. "Oh yes. She has as much money as an aristocrat. They say she has quite the head for business, which shouldn't be a woman's purview, but one *does* hear that the Irish are of a baser sort. Maybe their women are more like men."

Loath as I was to defend Molly in this moment, I felt a flash of ire. I'd heard whispers about my mother's heritage all my life. Irish, Scotch, Welsh—God forbid any of us *baser* sorts pollute Britannia. I focused on breathing, on feeling the wheels rattle underneath me, before I said something I regretted.

She went on. "Anyway, Mr. Markham hasn't had any guests—other than *you*—since his wife died. One might think it's a little, well, not done, to have such a party when his wife is barely cold in her grave."

"One might think, Mrs. Harold? Or you might think?"

She turned her head to look at me, giving me the look of someone who's just realized that they've underestimated an adversary. "What do you know about Violet Markham's death?" she dropped the overly friendly tone and switched into something more businesslike. "As her cousin, surely you must be interested."

"I must admit I don't know much."

"Let me tell you something then. Mr. Markham is dangerous. There isn't a villager in Stokeleigh who doesn't think he murdered Violet, and his first wife too."

"His first wife died of consumption."

Mrs. Harold waved a hand dismissively. "That's what killed her, yes, but that was just the method—he meant for her to die as soon as he married her. He never wanted to marry, you know. He traveled after his father died and the *stories* you'd hear about the things he got up to. But then the family lawyers convinced him to come back and to wed, to have a son because there are no longer any living relatives to be listed as inheritors. They practically picked a wife for him—Arabella Whitefield—and you couldn't have found a richer, more pedigreed girl anywhere. But she was frail— everyone knew that—she'd always been frail. Then he took her to Venice—hot, wet, rife with illness— for their honeymoon and she was so weakened by the travel and the weather that she immediately took sick."

"I think that sounds more like a tragic circumstance than intentional murder."

"You really think that a man in love, who knew his wife was sickly and weak, would subject her to such a journey? Would take her into such a warm, unhealthy climate? No. He wanted her to get sick. And don't even get me started on Violet. They fought from the moment she moved into Markham Hall." Her eyes were far down the path, and

102

something in her voice hinted at more substance than speculation. "And then she took up with Gareth the servant—who used to be such a nice boy—just to spite him. No wonder he snapped and decided to kill her."

"I'm not sure that qualifies as a certain evidence of homicide," I said, but inside I wondered...could Violet have really carried on an affair with Gareth? There was a possessiveness to Mr. Markham; perhaps he would be very angry indeed if he discovered his wife had been unfaithful. And our childhood curate had always said that sexual immorality bred other types of sin—perhaps a man so rife with the vice of lust would be rife with others...

"Certain evidence?" Mrs. Harold said. "How about this? The night before she died, they had a dinner party, and of course, my husband and I were invited. They were in rare form that night, fighting from the moment the meal started until the guests started leaving late that night. At one point, he pulled her out of the room, but we could still hear them quite clearly. He told her he'd have no shame divorcing her, and then *she* told him that she would never submit to a divorce and that he'd have to kill her if he wanted free. The next morning, she was cold in the field. And do you know what Mr. Markham did when he found her body? He laughed. He threw his head back and laughed."

This last comment gave me pause. The thought of him laughing next to Violet's corpse, shrouded in the fog, her neck at an unnatural angle—it made me deeply uncomfortable. It made me doubt whatever surety I'd felt about Mr. Markham's innocence. Who could laugh next to the body of his dead wife?

"How do you know?" I asked. "That he laughed?"

She pursed her lips, and a quick glance told me that I had struck upon something unexpected— information that Mrs. Harold was reluctant to share. "I spent the night at Markham Hall that night," she said. "I had taken ill shortly after dinner, and Mr. Markham extended his hospitality until I was recovered enough to journey home. That morning, I heard the servants talking about it."

"So the servants saw him in the field with Violet's body?"

"Yes," was the hesitant, cagey answer.

She was lying about something, or at least omitting part of the truth. But why?

We rolled up on Markham Hall, shaded and stony even in the bright sunlight, and I was surprised to see Mr. Markham striding towards us before Mrs. Harold had stopped the carriage. In the speckled light that drifted into the courtyard, I could see the faint highlights of gold hidden in his dark hair. He came up beside the carriage and, without a word, slid his hands around my waist and lifted me from the phaeton. He deposited me on the ground, keeping one arm firmly around me.

"Thank you for returning our Miss Leavold," he said, his voice clipped. "I'm much in your debt."

"Of course, Mr. Markham. Although she seemed to have wandered from the fold quite willingly." I couldn't quite decipher her tone—half-teasing, half-challenging, laced through with something else. Bitterness?

I looked at her as she squirmed under Mr. Markham's piercing gaze. It was the town gossip confronted with one of her subjects, the gossip feeling both shame and judgment, I decided. Of course, he wouldn't be unaware of the things she said about him.

Mr. Markham's arm tightened around me. "I'll have to keep a better eye on her in the future. Thank you again."

I knew the polite thing would be to invite Mrs. Harold inside for refreshments, but that didn't seem to be on Mr. Markham's agenda. He gave Mrs. Harold a short bow and then turned away, taking me with him and leaving her to drive herself home alone.

Chapter Ten

"What exactly did you think you were doing, wandering off alone? I had no idea where you were—"

"What I do with my day is none of your business." I shook off the arm that was still wrapped around my waist. We were in the foyer now, which was several degrees cooler than the outside, and much darker. A portrait of some indeterminate ancestor stared at us moodily, and a low murmur of conversation and laughter told me that the guests were in the drawing room nearby. Which meant that Molly would be nearby. I took a breath and lowered my voice. "I prefer not to spend the entire day indoors. Not in the summer. And you didn't seem to mind my exploring earlier in the week."

He softened. "You're right. I don't expect you to conform your day to my presence. But I woke up expecting you to be around and you weren't." He stepped closer. "I am just so used to getting what I want that when it doesn't happen, I don't know what to do with myself."

"I think it's a little unfair to want me to linger around you all day when…" I trailed off. He didn't know that I had overheard him and Molly last night and maybe it was better to keep it that way.

His eyes narrowed. "When what?"

"Nothing."

"Ivy…"

The sound of my Christian name on his lips was intimate, proprietorial. Suddenly, I wanted nothing more than to hear him say it, over and over again.

"Ah, hello you two," Silas said, exiting the drawing room. "Miss Leavold, I'm glad to see you've returned to us."

He took my hand and made to kiss it, but Mr. Markham stopped him with a firm hand on his shoulder. "That's enough."

"Enough what? I'm only being polite!" But his protestations were belied by his wide grin.

Mr. Markham merely shook his head and steered me into the drawing room. I didn't want to go, didn't want to see Molly O'Flaherty's pretty befreckled face after having heard her with Mr. Markham, but his hand was so warm on my back and the desire to be near him so urgent and overwhelming that I was doing as he bid even before I knew I was doing it.

The day passed in the warm torpour of the wealthily bored. There were half-hearted games of cards and suggested picnics or outings, a lazy lunch that dragged on for hours, lots of needlework that was picked up only to be immediately thrown to the side. And all the while, I made a point to avoid Molly and Mr. Markham, to avoid even looking at them, because I could not look at Mr. Markham's face without imagining what it looked like last night. Were his eyes closed when Molly kissed him? His cheeks flushed?

I felt my own face warm whenever these

thoughts intruded, and finally, an hour or so before dinner, I claimed a headache and went to my room. I tried to read, I tried to pace, nothing helped rid me of the twin burdens of desire and jealousy. One fed the other until I was entirely consumed by both.

A few hours passed and there was a knock at the door. Adrenaline shot through me—eagerness and fear—and I walked to the door as calmly as I could force myself, only to open it and find one of the lady's maids there. She handed me a note, curtsied and left.

It was from Mr. Markham. I sat down and unfolded it with slightly shaking hands.

I expect you to come down after dinner.
—J M

A thrill shot through me at this confirmation that he wanted my company, but at the same time, I felt a stab of irritation. I wasn't going to be at his beck and call, answering his every whim, not when he had Molly O'Flaherty to do it for him. And besides, I still felt somewhat outside of the group, left out of their jokes and their shared stories, a novice when it came to their libertine games.

I would go down, I decided, but not right away. I would put in an appearance later—sneak into the room while they were in the middle of some raucous diversion—and then leave shortly thereafter. As twistingly painful as it was to have witnessed Mr. Markham's—I couldn't say *betrayal* because I was not his to betray—interlude, then, I still needed to be around him. I hungered for just one glance, just one

108

word...one semi-accidental brush of hands or shoulders.

I chose a sapphire satin with a slightly fuller skirt and a neckline so low that I suspected if I were Catholic, I would need to be shriven after wearing it. I wore the black ribbon again since I owned no necklace or brooch to ornament the ensemble, made sure my hair was still adequately pinned, and then sat down to wait. I calculated that dinner would last at least a half hour more, and then it would be another half hour or hour after that when the men joined the ladies in the parlor.

A knock at the door interrupted my calculations. Probably another note reminding me that I needed to come down. I unlocked the door and opened it, finding not a maid but Mr. Markham himself. I stepped back in surprise but not before he stepped inside.

"I couldn't wait to see you. And I see you are already dressed," he said, pleased. "I like this one. Turn, please."

"I am not a mannequin in a shop window. You must contrive of ways to admire my figure discreetly, as other men must do."

"There's very little about me that is discreet, Miss Leavold," he said. "Suppose I were to *make* you turn." He placed his hands on my bare shoulders and spun me around, once slowly and then faster and faster.

There was dizziness and the beautiful dress swirling around my feet and the warmth of his hands on my shoulders, and a soft laugh escaped from me. When I finally came to a stop, I saw that Mr. Markham was smiling too, but once he saw my face, his expression stilled into something serious.

"Your eyes are sparkling," he said. "I wish you could see them as I see them right now. They are truly arresting."

I said nothing, and I couldn't have spoken even if I knew what to say because my breathing stuttered and my pulse raced.

His hands grew tight on my shoulders. "Ivy—"

"Well, aren't you a pair of lovebirds," Molly said from the doorway. I realized, too late, that we'd left the door open. Her voice was teasing but her eyes were—not hostile exactly—but sharply observant.

"Miss O'Flaherty." Mr. Markham's voice was cold. He released my shoulders with a stern admonition to come downstairs and then left the room, leaving Molly and me together.

She studied me, her eyes raking up and down my form in a manner no less lascivious than Mr. Markham's. She licked her lips. "You do look a treat tonight, Ivy. No wonder he couldn't keep his hands off you."

The jealousy unfolded in her presence, making itself larger and stronger and stifling my thoughts. "The dresses were his to choose," I managed to say politely enough. "It's only natural that they would be to his liking."

"Oh, but it's you that is to his liking, angel."

Molly stepped forward and drew a lazy finger across my cleavage. Gooseflesh pebbled along my skin. "Yes, quite nice," she said. "You know, dear old Jules asked us to stay away from you, said you'd had a hard enough life without us *corrupting* you. But you know what? I think you've earned a little fun after the life you've had. And besides—you are too tempting to resist."

And then she leaned forward and brushed her lips against my neck. I should have stepped back, should have pushed her away—the memory of her voice in the dark last night made my hands itch with the temptation—but then the sensation of her mouth on my skin was so delightful, so soft and entrancing, that I didn't. Her fingers continued to trace circles on my chest. "He wants you, you know."

"I know," I said. It was difficult to sound calm and collected while her tongue flicked unknowable patterns on my skin.

"He's saving you for himself. Selfish." She nipped at my collarbone and a noise escaped my throat. I could feel her lips curl into a smile, and she nipped again.

She pulled away and looked at me. I knew I was flushed, that my breath was coming faster, that my body didn't want her to stop.

"He'll have his way with you, you know. Eventually. He'll tease you and woo you and fuck you, and for a brief time, you'll be his, totally and completely. Until he grows bored."

There was bitterness in her voice. "Is that what

happened to you?" I asked.

"Oh no, poppet. I left him. See, no one leaves Molly O'Flaherty. Not even the handsome, tortured, impossibly rich Julian Markham. Not even him."

But what about last night? I wondered, but thought it best to keep pretending that I didn't know. "And how do you know I won't be the same?"

She looked at me a moment, cocking her head, blinking her jewel-bright eyes like a bird. "Interesting," she murmured. "I suppose I don't. See you downstairs then."

I did exactly as I had planned. I went downstairs and sat in the back of the parlor, barely noticed by anyone save Mr. Markham. Tonight they played Blind Man's Buff, taking turns being blindfolded and groping their way across the room, trying to bump into people and then guess their identity. Silas was dipping the people he caught into deep kisses, regardless of their gender, to the delight and merriment of all. Mr. Markham came near. "Will you have a turn?"

"Maybe later," I hedged, knowing I would escape before then and I very nearly did, making my way out of the parlor some twenty minutes later. But Mr. Markham followed me.

"You are not enjoying yourself," he said.

"I am," I said. "I'm merely tired."

He bit his lip, looking very young for a moment. "Molly said that she talked to you upstairs. About me."

112

There was no point in denying it. "Yes."

"You know, I am denying myself—denying them—because I feel like I should protect you."

"Protect me from what?" I demanded. "I have no future, I have no family. I no longer have a home. What consequence could my behavior possibly have at this point? You must know that I will never marry, not without money or any connections." I pressed my hands against his chest and he breathed in. "My body belongs only to me now. And I want to do with it what I will."

I expected him to reply, but instead he lifted me and placed me on a low table against the wall, pressing his lips against mine. They tasted sweet, of dessert wine and cloves, and when he made to part my lips with his, I allowed him, relishing his warmth and his taste. But the noises we made, the breathing and the soft whisper of lips parting and meeting—it sounded too much like last night. Something stabbed in my chest.

"You and Molly—"

He froze and pulled back. "What else did she say to you?" he demanded.

"Nothing—"

"Tell me," he said, and his voice had lost any warmth it might have had. It was a command, and suddenly I pictured how it would sound to him, me being hurt over something that was his prerogative and none of my business.

"Molly said you would make me yours and then abandon me," I said instead.

He looked hard at me. "She doesn't—"

I pressed a finger against his lips. "What I'm saying is that I don't care. I want you, no matter what happens to me afterwards."

"Molly doesn't know what she's talking about," he said. "I would never abandon you. And regardless, we will never need to find out. I *will* restrain myself." He pushed himself away from me, eyes full of resolve.

"But that's not fair!" I cried. "You touch me, you make me want things only you can give, and now you withdraw yourself completely? What about me? What about what I want?"

He sighed. "I'm trying to help you."

I glanced around the hallway to make sure we were alone then I reached down with one hand and pulled up the silk dress and the petticoats underneath and spread my legs. Mr. Markham's eyes darkened with lust. I took his hand and slid it up my thigh. "Then *help me*. I want you all the time. I think of you all the time. My body burns and aches and…"

"And you are so wet," Mr. Markham growled, sliding a finger inside of me. His thumb began pressing against my clit. "Look at us, Ivy. I could fuck you on this table right now."

He was right. I looked down and saw that his pelvis was perfectly aligned with mine. If he drew himself out of his pants, he'd have only to part my folds with his cock and push in…the thought made my pulse pound.

"But I won't," he finished, pulling his finger out

114

of me.

I practically wilted.

He closed his eyes a moment. "You are right that your body is your own. And perhaps Molly is right that you should be included in their games. She's been trying to persuade me ever since she got here that there was no sense in denying you. Perhaps as long as things do not go too far...would you like to play with the others?"

"Play?"

He opened his eyes. "What they were playing earlier. Blind Man's Buff."

I hardly saw how that would alleviate my current discomfort, but I said, "If that is what you would like."

"I think you'll find that it is what *you* would like."

Chapter Eleven

"Miss Leavold is going to play with us," Mr. Markham announced as we entered the room once more.

The girls clapped their hands delightedly.

"But I must set down some rules," he continued.

The girls pouted. He gave them a stern look.

"Gather round. No, not you Miss Leavold. Wait over there."

They clustered around Mr. Markham, talking in low murmurs, while I stood uncomfortably by myself, feeling excluded from their conference and also feeling trepidatious about the contents of it at the same time. He had said we were going to play Blind Man's Buff—what could there be to talk about?

The group dispersed and Ned came over to tie the blindfold around my head, knotting it securely. I could hear the people moving about the room, finding hiding spots behind furniture and curtains.

A cool glass pressed against my mouth. "It's only wine," Ned said. "To help you relax."

That didn't sound so bad. I parted my lips and drank as Ned held the glass for me.

"Have you ever played before?" he asked.

"As a child."

I could hear the smile in his voice. "Our rules are a little different. You'll see. But the premise is the same—search for the others. If you can name the person you've captured, then they are out of the game. If you cannot name them, then they are free to escape. Are you ready?"

"I suppose."

"Well then. Best of luck, Miss Leavold." And Ned's warm presence was gone.

With the blindfold obscuring my sight, my other senses heightened. I could still taste the wine on my lips, feel the heat from the nearby fire on my back. Shoes shuffled on the carpet as I took a tentative step forward. I could hear the rustling of gowns, the occasional giggle and the ensuing *shh*.

I reached out a hand, following the noise, using my memory as best I could to navigate around the furniture. My fingertips grazed something—a sleeve—the sleeve of a dinner jacket—and I seized the arm within it and pulled its owner close. I reached up to touch their face, to make an identification, and then I felt lips pressed against mine. Not Mr. Markham's lips—these were fuller, gentler. I felt myself tense under the unexpected touch—Mr. Markham was watching and I felt some sort of loyalty to him, however misguided that loyalty was.

"It's okay," the person whispered. "It's part of the game."

The Gallic accent gave him away. "Hugh?" I guessed.

"One for Miss Leavold," I heard Helene say.

I kept walking, bolstered by this little victory.

Arms out, fingers flexed, I ran right into a woman who smelled of something spicy and exotic. I wondered if she would kiss me too, but instead, she wrapped her fingers around mine and placed them against her chest, sliding them down from her breasts to the nip of her waist and then the swell of her hips. The embroidery on her dress scratched against my palms. Who had been wearing an embroidered dress?

"Adella?"

"I am Charlotte," she said with a throaty giggle.

"What's the verdict, Markham?" someone asked.

"Relieve her of it," he answered.

And then a couple pairs of hands spun me around and started tugging at my dress.

"Wait—" I protested feebly.

"Our rules, sweetie," Molly said from nearby. "Every wrong guess costs you one article of clothing. And the dress counts as one."

Hooks were unfastened, bustles unhooked, and suddenly the dress was pulled up above my head and cast aside. I now wore only my corset and petticoats with a very low-cut and thin chemise underneath them. I shivered—partly from the feeling of air brushing against my shoulders but also from a feeling of excitement. The knot in my belly tied itself anew, tightening itself at the unexpected thrill of being exposed before so many, and at Mr. Markham's behest.

I caught another woman next, and this one did

kiss me, parting my lips with her soft ones. She pressed her body against mine, and even through my corset and her clothes, I could feel her curves.

"Ettie," I said confidently.

"Hmph," she said, pulling away. Another point for me. And so it went for two more turns, until I came upon a man. Not Mr. Markham—I would know him blindfolded, deafened, and deprived of touch. This man was slightly taller. And rather than kiss me, he took my hand and brought it to the front of his breeches.

"How am I supposed to tell from this?" I said, a little bit indignantly and to the great mirth of the onlookers. "Owen?" I guessed.

"Silas," he replied and then my hand was inside his breeches and he curled my fingers around his quickly stiffening cock. "Maybe before I leave, I can make the memory of this so indelible that you'll never lose a game again."

I withdrew my hand, feeling Mr. Markham's gaze even while blindfolded, and Silas clucked in disappointment. "What shall she have off then?"

"The petticoats!" the others cried.

"Just one," I said, "just one!"

But all three came off. "They really work together as one unit," Silas explained. He was the one who reached his arms around my waist to untie them and pull them down over my hips. I was now only in my stockings, corset and chemise, which came down to the middle of my thighs.

"I do feel less impeded now," I said to the

general amusement of the room, and I found myself much less self-conscious than I would have imagined, being so exposed. It must have been the wine.

The next person I caught was Molly—I knew it by her slender figure and the familiar way she nipped at my neck. But after that, I mistook Adella for Helene, and lost my corset. Adella herself unlaced it, quickly and deftly, and I felt my breasts released as she pulled it off me. They felt swollen, ripe, and the sensation of the now-loose chemise brushing against my nipples was enough to make me shudder.

"Oh!" Adella exclaimed, pulling up the chemise to expose my backside. *"Regardez-vous,"* she ordered the others. *"Très délicieux."*

She ran a finger up my thigh and I jumped, moving away from her. "Now, now," Silas reproved. "You'll frighten our little deer."

I had no sense of distance without my vision, but I moved fairly quickly away from Adella and ran right into someone tall and lean, someone who steadied me with calloused fingers on my arms. This time, I initiated a kiss, knowing it was Mr. Markham, and wanting nothing more than to press my body against his and feel his skin against mine.

"I know you," I breathed against him.

"Well, by all means, hide it from the others and guess incorrectly." His hands slid down my hips. "It's time for this to come off." He rucked up the chemise.

"Not a chance," I said. "I intend to win. I've caught you."

"I think you'll find, wildcat, that I've caught you." And then he tugged the chemise up and over, sliding it off me with an ease that suggested practice with a lady's underthings. I was now naked, save for the stockings, blindfolded and completely helpless. I should have felt embarrassed or frightened, I should have wanted to dart away. But I didn't.

I did reach up for the blindfold, thinking that the game must be finished now, but Mr. Markham caught my hands and stopped me. "Not yet," he murmured.

He kissed my bare neck, letting his mouth graze over my collarbone and over to my shoulder. I shivered. And then I felt warm hands on my back—more than two.

Then there were lips on my back, along my calves and on the outside of my thighs. Mr. Markham guided me back until I was on the plush rug by the fire. The blindfold made every sensation seem magnified, sharper, and I could feel the heat of the flames on one side of me, and the cool rug beneath me, feel the fingertips that began to trail along my arms and legs. There were too many to tell which belonged to whom, and I could feel the rougher skin of the men alongside the soft hands of the women.

And then Mr. Markham was kissing me again, his mouth claiming mine. He was braced on his arms above me, his jacket hanging down and

brushing against the sensitive skin of my nipples. I
arched my back, and he moved down, his lips
searing a path from my breasts to my navel. My legs
parted instinctively as he kissed down to the swell of
my pubic bone, and an unfamiliar hand brushed over
my breast, squeezing it, rolling my nipple between
slender, deft fingers, making me whimper.

Mr. Markham opened his mouth, his tongue hot
and lashing, and then there were more hands and
lips—kissing my neck, stroking my hair. I gasped as
someone took my nipple into their mouth, sucking
hard, and Julian continued to pass his tongue over
the same spot, and then he slid his finger inside of
me, and I wished it was more, I wished it was so
much more, but at the same time, it was all too
much, the hands and the mouths and crashing tide
inside of me.

"Look," I heard Molly say, "she's about to
come."

A finger followed the heat as it spread up my
body, up to my stomach and into my chest, and then
two hands clamped down on my hips to keep them
from bucking.

"Oh," I breathed. "Oh."

"She's such a pretty pet when she's writhing,"
Molly said. "Aren't you ready to have her
underneath you, Julian?"

"Don't tempt me," he said roughly, the breath
from his words blowing against my wet center, and
then he slid another finger inside of me. I tried to
buck harder, and then his mouth was on me again,

and then I crashed, tremors roiling through me, my back arching so far off the floor that I could feel the air flowing underneath it. The waves slowed and settled, leaving me limp and warm-feeling.

"A fine prologue," Silas said. "But it is time for the main act."

I reached for the blindfold again, but I was stopped once more. Mr. Markham slid an arm underneath my knees and back and lifted me, carrying me somewhere. We only went a handful of steps, and I could still hear all the guests, so I knew that we were still in the parlour. Mr. Markham sat, bringing me down to his lap. I sat facing out, still naked, and Mr. Markham spread my legs, his fingers once again finding my pussy, now swollen and slick.

"The others are playing now," he whispered in my ear. "Would you like to know what they are doing?"

I nodded. His fingers had already found the tenderest part of me; he was rubbing in slow, light circles.

"They are watching as Silas undresses Molly," he said very quietly. "He's pulled off her dress and now he's working on her corset—there goes her chemise. She's almost completely naked now. Silas is kissing her—her lips and now her breasts and now he's kissing her cunt. She likes that—she likes that very much."

I could hear Molly's gasps as Silas continued his ministrations. I made a gasp of my own when Mr. Markham slid a finger inside of me.

"Molly is impatient, just like you. She's undressing Silas now, he's letting her, and now she's on top of him, sliding herself against his cock."

I could feel Mr. Markham's own hardness beneath me, could feel him respond whenever I ground against him.

"And now he's grabbed her hips and pushed himself inside of her."

Molly's moans filled the parlor. I could hear the noises of others—heavy breathing, groans, and the sound of skin on skin.

"Everyone has joined in now," Mr. Markham said softly. I turned towards him.

"Shall we?" I asked.

"No, Miss Leavold." But his voice was ragged. Losing control.

"Please," I said. "Please…just a little bit."

"*No.*" This time his voice was more forceful. He picked me up once more and carried me out of the room.

"Where are you taking me?" I demanded. He had stirred me once again, right after that first climax, and my body clamored for more. I wasn't finished yet. I squirmed and kicked to get down, and then I was pinned up against the wall, the wooden paneling cold on my bare back.

"What are you doing?" I breathed, feeling every line of his body through his clothes, feeling his hips pressed against mine.

He didn't answer, but his lips were on my neck, hot and scorching, and then he reached down and unbuttoned his trousers. He hooked an arm around my leg, raising it up, and then I could feel the hot length of his cock pressing against me, hard and urgent.

I slid my hands through his hair and then pulled his head back so that I could kiss him. The blindfold kept everything in complete darkness—reducing everything to sounds and touch—but that was all I needed, because at that moment, the head of his cock pressed up against my folds, and I thought I would never need any other sensation again. I could live forever with only this feeling—the blindfold silky against my eyes, his dinner jacket soft on my breasts, his wide crown slowly, oh so slowly, pushing in, caressing me, separating me.

"Oh, wildcat," he moaned, his head buried once again in my shoulder. "Oh, God. You feel so good. Make me stop. Make me stop." He pushed further in and I gasped.

"Don't stop," I begged.

We stayed there for a long moment, me pinned against the wall, his breath against my neck, his cock barely inside of me. I could feel every heartbeat, every pulse, and all I wanted was for him to finish it, to thrust all the way inside, and fuck me against this wall, right where anyone in the house could see.

With a throaty exhalation, he pulled away, his lips leaving my neck, his hips parting from mine.

"No," he said again, and he finally sounded in control of his voice. "I can't."

I had a litany of protestations, of reasons why it

125

was okay and *right* even, but then I felt the blindfold removed from my face. I looked at him for the first time in an hour, seeing the flush to his cheeks and the brightness to his eyes. He'd buttoned his pants once more, but a rigid outline was still visible. I reached for it but he grabbed my wrist.

"Go to bed," he said.

"I'm not ready."

He was breathing hard still, but his voice was steady as his eyes burned into mine. "Shall I wrestle you to bed, then?"

I didn't answer, because I knew the answer was apparent in my face and eyes and in the way I arched my back to press against him. He let go of me and took a step back.

"Goodnight," he said, and then he left me, naked and wanting, in the hallway.

Chapter Twelve

I woke early that next day, before the sun, before any of the guests—some of whom were still in the parlour, sleeping in a tangled mess of limbs and silk. My heart pulled remembering last night; it had been both delicious and painful.

I only knew one thing—I had to see Mr. Markham. I had to talk to him, had to touch him. He'd invaded my dreams and my waking mind—a thought would arise, only to be chased away by the memory of his lips on my skin, of his hardness slowly pressing inside of me. It was like a disease, falling in love with him, and it made me apathetic and anxious all at the same time.

I went down to the kitchen to find an early breakfast. Wispel was grumbling around a table, gathering eggs and onions into bowls. "No doubt going to sleep late again, not so much as a hint as to when they'll want breakfast, and I'm not a magician, I can't pull a full breakfast out of thin air at a whim."

Whether she was complaining to me or I had simply arrived in the middle of an ongoing soliloquy, I didn't know.

"Would it be okay if I had something to take with me for breakfast? I'm thinking of going outdoors to eat."

Wispel shook her head. "You and the master, both up hours before the others, both wanting separate meals. There's only one of me, you know, at least until the village girls get here to help with luncheon and supper."

"Mr. Markham is already awake?" My heart jumped. I might be able to see him, alone and apart from any of the others. "Is he still in the house?"

"He also wanted to be outside. I think he had a letter to post in the village. Couldn't get his valet to do it, like a normal master, oh no." And despite her grumbling, Wispel pulled together a bundle of warm bread and hard cheese and two hardboiled eggs.

I took the bundle gratefully, eager to get outside and find Mr. Markham. Wispel must have noticed, because she kept her hand on the food for a moment. "It does not do to follow men about," she warned me. "The late mistress was much the same way before she married, and it only sowed unhappiness for her."

For whatever reason, I didn't feel defensive or chagrined—Wispel seemed kind enough in her intentions. I did, however, remember my conversation with Mrs. Harold yesterday—the one where she'd accused Mr. Markham of killing not one, but two wives.

"Thank you," I told her, and then left the kitchens, my thoughts floating away from kisses in the dark and floating towards sabotaged saddles and gravestones. And so I turned my feet toward the village, knowing now where I'd go.

The lingering shadows seemed to hug the village church longer than any other building, and so the churchyard still had an air of night about it, even

128

though the main street was now washed with the rosy oranges of dawn.

I walked through the sagging wooden lych-gate into the graveyard, picking my way around sunken graves and crooked gravestones, looking for a newer grave. I wanted to find Violet. It was something I should have done as soon as I'd come, but my thoughts and energy had been so occupied with her widower that I hadn't. That surely made me a terrible cousin, but if she'd been alive, she might not have minded. Violet herself had always put men first.

The graveyard wrapped around the church, the grass impossibly green and the stones speckled with moss and lichen, and then I found Violet's grave without even needing to scan the headstones. Mr. Markham was standing beside it, his eyes fixed on the stone, his hands behind his back.

I was unsure whether to approach or not, but then he said, without looking over at me, "Join me, Miss Leavold."

I did, all the while thinking of Mrs. Harold and Wispel and their stories. Even though I craved his presence and his touch, I came around the other side of the grave, keeping my eyes on Mr. Markham.

"You look at me so warily," he said, again keeping his eyes fixed on the stone. He gave the impression of someone who could see everything. "Are you worried I'm going to bite?"

I didn't answer at first. It was strange having Violet's grave actually before me, actually between us, it was strange and terrifying but it felt inevitable as well. That if he were to kiss me again, we should be here in this gloomy place, staring at her name carved so cleanly into the white marble. Atop the plinth was a pale angel, her hands covering her face, her head bent, perhaps in sorrow or perhaps in shame.

Whose sorrow? Whose shame?

"Did you really laugh when you found her?" I asked Mr. Markham. "When you found Violet dead?"

He finally looked up, his face serious. "What are you talking about?"

"After Violet died, and you were the first to find her—I heard that you laughed."

"No," he said softly.

"No, you didn't laugh?"

"No, I wasn't the first to find her."

The breeze blew through the yard and I shivered. "What do you mean?"

"I mean that there were footprints in the frost. Someone found her first and left her body there, without going to find help from anybody else."

"And then you laughed?"

His eyes flashed. "What are you implying? That I was happy when Violet died? That's a very sinister accusation, Miss Leavold."

"I'm not accusing you of anything," I said.

"Yet how carefully you keep your distance."

Because you frighten me. And he did, in that moment. His anger was palpable, as was some

130

darkness that roiled within him, and at the same time that part of my brain signaled me to step backward, another part of me remembered that I was dependent on him for everything—for shelter and food and almost every portion of my well being. I needed to remain sensible of that—that no matter how I loved him or how I feared him, I still relied on his goodwill and benevolence.

"I shouldn't have disturbed you," I said. "I'll leave you now."

"Don't," he said.

I chafed at the order, yet I obeyed.

"I want you here with me, Miss Leavold," he said. "Violet was your family too. You should be able to pay your respects alongside her former husband."

And so we stayed at the grave another ten minutes, me looking at Mr. Markham from underneath my eyelashes, watching his face as he traced the lines of the angel with his eyes. There was longing in his expression and pain too, and his shoulders, normally so broad and straight, were slumped, as if a great weight were pressing down on him.

"I made a mistake once," he said. "And now its ghost will follow me forever."

Violet. Was his mistake in killing her? Or marrying her in the first place?

He looked up, searching my eyes. "You have something about her right now, in your face. I can see her, as if she's inside of you, wanting to speak to me."

"I feel nothing but myself," I said.

He came around the grave. "Perhaps you're right," he said. And then a finger traced up my sleeve to my neck, running down my jaw to my chin, where he held my face as he examined me. "I believe it is only Ivy Leavold inside of here."

For a moment, his face was mere inches from mine, and I could see every irregular fleck of pale jade in his bright green eyes. My body pulsed with heat, remembering last night.

"Would it be wrong of me to kiss you here?" he asked.

"Yes," I whispered.

"Then perhaps we should leave." He offered me an arm, and I took it, only looking back at the grave once as we made our way back to the house.

"It's supposed to be the party of the decade," Adella was telling the dinner table. "We can't miss it."

"The Prince of Wales will be there," Gideon added.

"Of course we're going," Molly said matter-of-factly. "It won't be any trouble to get down there by Friday, certainly."

"You'd want to leave tomorrow at the latest," Mr. Markham said. "Give yourself two days for the journey—it will be easier."

"You talk as if you aren't coming with us, Jules." Molly glanced over at me as she said it, as if it were my fault.

"I've been to one of the baron's parties, and once was enough for me."

"Perhaps you were at the wrong party," Silas said, grinning. "Because everyone knows that once is never enough. And you haven't been down to London in over two months—for all you know, your house there has been burgled and all the servants have given up on you ever coming back and left."

Mr. Markham picked up his wine glass. "I doubt that."

"Oh, do come with us," Helene said. "Why would you stay here in this dreary old heap when we can stay at the Savoy and dance with royalty?"

"Thank you, Helene, but my mind is quite made up." Our eyes met for the briefest of moments and then he looked back at the others. "I've left Markham Hall too unattended as of late, and I must set myself to my responsibilities. For a little while at least."

I kept my gaze on my plate, trying not to give any indication of how happy this made me, that Mr. Markham was staying here, and that I would have him to myself once again.

Molly was clearly not pleased. "Don't cloister yourself, Jules. It never makes you happy. You're not meant to be stationary and domestic."

"You know me not at all if you think that I am at risk of being domestic."

She didn't answer, but there was something sharp in her face as she turned to Charlotte and struck up a conversation. Something sharp and savage, and I knew that this seemingly small transgression of Mr. Markham's would not be forgotten.

They left the next morning, in a flurry of trunks and carriages and frantic servants, the guests yawning widely and rubbing their eyes as they climbed into their conveyances.

I was kissed and petted by the women and given deep, stately bows from the men, and they all exclaimed over how much they would miss me while they were gone. I treated these sentiments politely but skeptically. I failed to see how they could form such an attachment to me in a matter of days, but perhaps some people were like that, seeking transient thrills and connections and people, and perhaps they really felt as if we had formed some sort of insoluble bond since they'd arrived. Then I flushed, remembering the night in the parlour, the lips and the hands, all stroking and caressing and rubbing, and the way I'd given myself over to it entirely, the pleasure and the fitful ecstasy of such intimate things.

Silas gave me a lingering kiss on the cheek. "Goodbye, pet," he said. "I look forward to seeing you again." He leaned closer, his lips brushing against my ear. "And I look forward to tasting you again." He pulled back, his blue eyes burning, and my body warmed in response.

Then he gave a wide smile—all white teeth and

charm. "That is, if Mr. Markham ever decides to share you again."

"Don't bother the girl, Silas," Molly said, coming up to us. She looked very smart in a light blue traveling dress and matching bonnet.

"I'm not bothering her," Silas said. "I'm making promises."

"To the carriage." Molly waved him off. "Honestly." He gave me a bow and then left, the grin subsiding into something like a smirk, as if he were pondering a private joke.

Molly looked at me in that half-quizzical, half-razored way of hers. "We will be back after our stay in London, I'm sure," she said. "It is so strange that Julian should stay home. Normally, he would never miss a chance to escape this place. I must conclude that it has something to do with you."

"Mr. Markham makes his own decisions for his own reasons," I said.

"Oh my dear," Molly said. "You are so bad at hiding your feelings. Don't be ashamed—I doubt you've had practice with it. I can see in your eyes that you want him and that he wants you. It will only be a matter of time now. But don't forget what I told you—Julian Markham will make you his world, but only for a time. Are you strong enough to bear that kind of disappointment?"

"You know nothing of my strength," I said, unexpectedly irritated. "And beyond that, it's none of your business."

She cocked her head at me. "I'm not your

enemy, Ivy. You are young and not used to the games of grown men. I only want to help."

It was difficult for me to take her at her word when I could still hear the sounds of her and Mr. Markham together. "Then I should thank you for your consideration and courtesy."

She narrowed her eyes at me. "There's no need to be so cold."

Mr. Markham came over then, having supervised the loading of the trunks and hatboxes. "Miss O'Flaherty," he said, inclining his head.

"Julian." She raised her hand and he kissed it quickly and then dropped it.

"Safe journey," he said and then placed a hand at the small of my back to guide me back to the door.

"See you soon," Molly called as she climbed into the carriage. Mr. Markham didn't answer, but I knew that he'd heard.

She gave me a smile through the carriage window as it rolled away, a smile both menacing and pretty at the same time, and I knew that whatever was between us would never be friendship. She had her own agenda, her own desires, and she was far more experienced than me at seeing her desires flower into fruit.

The last carriage creaked down the drive, and then it was only Mr. Markham and me. He gave me a look, long and intense, and he opened his mouth to speak, but then he turned back to the house and went inside. I remained in the courtyard, watching the trees blow in the summer wind, thinking of marble angels and Molly O'Flaherty.

Chapter Thirteen

That night, it was only Mr. Markham and myself for dinner. We sat with the table between us—an expanse of wood that felt painfully large, with silver tureens and carafes and tiered trays making it impossible to see one another, and hovering servants that made it awkward to converse. When it was time to adjourn to the parlour, I felt a heavy sense of relief. I wanted him alone, with nothing between us.

When he walked into the parlour, turning to shut the door quietly behind him, I came forward from the fireplace where I'd been standing.

"Ivy," he said, and the way he said my name was beautiful. It was music in an opera hall, rain on a lake, the first glorious birdsongs of early spring.

"Julian," I whispered.

Something thawed in his face, some darkness parted, and his eyes shone. "I like hearing that word from your lips."

"I like saying it. Very much." I came closer. "Why did you stay?"

"For you."

A nervous sort of joy flipped in my stomach.

Now it was he who took a step closer. "I stayed for you, Ivy. I stayed because I wanted you all to myself. The others were right, I'm hoarding you, but I can't help it. I want your time and your conversation and your company. And your—" here his voice caught.

"…And my body," I finished for him.

"Yes. And that."

"I am glad you didn't go," I whispered. But I couldn't bear it any longer. "What happened between you and Molly O'Flaherty?"

"History," he answered after a moment. "Ancient history."

"But…"

Understanding kindled in his eyes. "You heard us. The night we played charades."

I nodded, my throat stupidly tight.

"I didn't fuck her," he said. "If that's what you thought."

"I heard kissing." My voice quavered, and I inwardly cursed my weakness. I wanted to be sophisticated and aloof about this. I wanted him to see how strong I could be. But I cared too much. Hurt too much.

I wanted him all to myself.

"She kissed me," he admitted. "And I kissed her back. I wanted you so badly, but I was also determined not to take advantage of you. She knew it. I think in her own way she was trying to help."

"She's still in love with you."

He laughed. "Molly doesn't love people. She may desire them, she may enjoy their company, but she would never stoop to the level of such an undignified emotion."

"But you two were together once."

"Once," he said. "But no more. I pushed her

away that night you heard us. I don't indulge in inferior consolation. If I couldn't have you, then I wouldn't have anyone." He turned away from me for a moment, half his face in shadow. "And I needed to be faithful to you. *I had to be.*"

The conviction in his voice was almost chilling in its intensity. It was the conviction of a sinner desperate to repent. I didn't understand it, but at the moment, I didn't care. I was too relieved.

"So you and Molly didn't..."

He faced me again. "No, wildcat. I couldn't. When I want someone the way I wanted—*want*—you, I don't fuck other women."

I shouldn't ask, but I couldn't help it. "Was it the same with Violet?"

He sunk into a chair. I got the sense that he was gathering his thoughts, preparing his words, and when he spoke, it was carefully. "I didn't sleep with anyone while I courted Violet. Not even her. God help me, I had this idea that if I didn't have her until we were married, that it would show her how different I was from the other men who wanted her, who kept chasing her even after she was engaged to me."

"Did it work?"

"In the end? No. There was no happy ending for us, and there wouldn't have been even if she had lived." He stood and starting pacing, running a hand through his hair. "There are things about me—things that frightened her, things that I could never even show my first wife—and you know what's strange?

I can show them to you. I feel like I can share the darkest parts of me, and you, little wildcat, would love it." He stopped in front of me, taking my wrist in his hand and bringing it to his mouth, kissing the delicate skin there. "You have the same darkness, I think. And that's what I need."

"And that wasn't Violet?"

His eyes darkened again. "No. That wasn't Violet." He let go of my wrist. "Imagine a exotic animal, captured from its native climate and then placed in a zoo. Imagine that animal grew sleek and lazy, spoiled and passive, still bearing the stripes or spots of a wild beast, but inside so feckless and tamed that weakness had permeated every lineament of its soul."

"Tamed is not a word I would have thought to describe Violet."

"Of course not—she gave every appearance to the contrary. But in the end, she was no different than any other well-bred girl who dabbles in lust. She wanted things soft and easy, the way most men were willing to give it to her."

"And what do you do that's so disturbing to these well-bred girls?"

"Would you like me to show you?"

"Yes," I said, all my doubts replaced with unconditional longing for the man in front of me. "Yes, again and again."

Mr. Markham took my hands in his own and looked at me. The firelight flickered off his square jaw and chiseled cheekbones, his eyes greener than ever. "You remember what I said in the library that night. I don't want to ruin you."

My face flushed hot, and I yanked my hands out of his. "You don't get to decide if I'm ruined, Julian Markham. I've spent the last ten years looking after myself. I'm as free as you are, and I get to decide whether something ruins my future or not."

"Ivy—"

"*I have no future*," I said. "I will never marry well, not with my family history and not with my lack of money. My only future is here, at Markham Hall. Unless you don't want me."

His eyes flashed. "Don't utter those words again."

"Then what is at stake, Mr. Markham? Truly?"

He seized my waist and pulled me close against him. "My soul. Yours."

Something about the desperate note in his voice made my blood flare, and I tilted my chin up, remembering the night we met, of the rasp in his words as he had taken my wrist in his hand. "My soul was yours to take from the moment I met you, Julian."

With a low growl, he swept me into his arms and carried me out of the parlour, his eyes glittering in the dark of the stairwell as he carried me to his bedchamber. My pulse was racing, lust and adrenaline and disbelief and—yes, if I admitted to myself, the smallest trace of fear—but when the flickering firelight of Mr. Markham's room threw his face into dim relief, I had never seen him look

142

calmer. He set me down on the thick rug before the hearth, staring at me as he shrugged off his dinner jacket and unknotted his cravat.

The intensity of his gaze unnerved me, and I took a step backward toward the door, not because I didn't want this, didn't want him, but because I knew beyond a doubt that everything in my life was about to change, completely and totally.

"Don't be skittish," he said, holding out a hand.

If I took it, then I was giving him my consent. I was giving myself consent. All of the conclusions I'd come to about our relationship, about our future, about what I wanted—tonight would cement them. This moment was my last chance to withdraw, to plumb any uncertainties I had left. Was I truly ready to give my body to this man in such an irrevocable manner?

I placed my hand in his, and he pulled me close, his lips brushing against my ear. "Do you trust me?"

Any well-brought up woman would say no. But I wasn't well-brought up, hadn't been anything remotely like that since my parents died. "Yes," I whispered.

"Good."

His hands slid down over my shoulders to my waist, and he dropped a kiss on my lips. I tilted my face toward him, wanting more, but he moved around behind me, and I felt his fingers dance down my neck, down to the hollow between my shoulder blades where the buttons to my dress began. One by one, the buttons tugged and loosened, freeing me incrementally.

The dress slid down my body, the silk whispering against my petticoats and my corset. "A woman's first time should be entirely about her," he said in a low voice. "I promise to do my best, but you test every limit of my self-control."

Oh, how I hoped that was true. I knew I should expect gentleness, but that wasn't ever what I had responded to from Julian. Seeing him at the edge of his restraint, his eyes half-lidded as he barely resisted his own darkest urges, knowing it was me who made him that way, it made me just as wild. I craved that, that simultaneous feeling of power and lack of power.

"Don't be too gentle," I murmured.

"With you, wildcat, I don't think there's any real risk of that."

My petticoats fell away, and he laid them carefully over a chair. Then came my corset, my breasts feeling heavy and full without its support.

When I was entirely naked, he stood before me, his eyes taking in every dip and curve of my body. I felt his eyes like his fingers, as if he were marking with his gaze all of the places he wanted to kiss. And I saw clearly the outline of his desire, his erection large and hard in his breeches. His eyes kept lingering on my breasts, on the place between my legs.

"You were made for fucking," he said roughly.

I looked at his green eyes, the way his body exuded power and wealth and lust and raw animal need.

"I was made for *you*," I answered.

In less than a second, his mouth was on mine, lips insistent and demanding. My lips parted and our tongues met, his hand behind my neck as we kissed. Even weeks after our first kiss, the connection still made my pulse pound and my body respond in ways that made any memory of propriety laughable.

Mr. Markham bent his lips to my neck, licking and nipping and sucking, and then—without warning—he swept an arm behind my knees and I was being carried to his bed. He kept kissing me as he walked, deeply and urgently, as if he couldn't help himself, as if he were desperate to taste as many kisses as he could.

"Close your eyes," he said as he laid me down. "I want you to think only about yourself."

But that was impossible. As his mouth closed over my nipple, drawing it into a stiff point, all I could think about was him—his face as he worshipped my breasts, the shadows in his eyes as he held himself back from the depths of his own desire. The sight of his erection, throbbing for me and me alone.

He moved to the other breast, and I moaned out loud. He lifted his head. "If you keep making noises like that, I won't be able to stop myself from taking you right now."

That was exactly what I wanted, and I meant to say so, but then his fingers brushed against my center and my words were lost. He petted, he played and he teased, until my hips were pushing up against his hand, begging and begging.

He moved his mouth down, kissing a circle around my navel, until he reached my mound, which he blanketed with soft kisses. The first time his tongue swept across my clitoris, I thought I would weep. His tongue caressed me again, slowly at first, then in quick flutters, punctuated by kisses further down, where he'd lick inside of me. And then gently, so gently that I didn't realize it was happening, his finger slipped inside of me. As he continued sucking on my clit, his finger crooked in just the right way, pressing against a place that made me buck my hips and pant. And then there were two fingers pressing, and his mouth hot and sucking, tongue dancing, and the knowledge that in a matter of moments he would be buried inside of me.

I came.

Waves of pleasure rolled through me, and he kept his mouth on me the whole time, not pulling away until my body had entirely stilled. He straightened up and ran his fingers down my torso, parting my legs with his hands so that I was all spread out for him. His jaw was working and his face was flushed, and I knew it was taking everything he had not to rush. He unbuttoned his shirt and pulled it off, throwing it to the floor without looking where it landed, and then he unbuttoned his trousers, freeing his thickness, which jutted out proudly from his narrow hips.

Through all the times he'd touched me, and I

him, I had never seen him naked. And the sight was impossibly perfect: his tall body banded with slender muscles, his stomach flat, his legs powerful and long. And his cock—though I had seen it before, felt it before, I was still mesmerized by it. By its thickness and length, by the wide crest of its crown. My body warmed once more at the thought of it touching me and penetrating me, but my mind also registered a dim nervousness.

"You're so big," I whispered.

He didn't answer my unspoken question. "Do you trust me?" he asked again.

I nodded, biting my lip. He crawled over me, his cock brushing against my stomach as he leaned down to take my lips. My taste still lingered on him, and I marveled at that—I was tasting myself and him at the same time. He stretched his body over mine, and I felt the unmistakable heat and hardness of him brush against my pussy.

My breath hitched. I'd only been this close to him once before, in the hallway a few nights ago, when he'd almost lost the war against himself and taken me up against the wall. The firelight flickered along his body, casting soft tessellations of light over his wide shoulders and powerful arms, and I looked down to see how his body looked over mine, poised to make it his own. The sight made me shudder. It was so sinful, so wrong. Never had I felt more at his mercy, and never had I felt more aroused.

He moved again, and again I felt his cock against me, but it was no longer light and teasing, but pressing. As I watched, my breath stitching uneven patterns, he took himself in his hand and rubbed his crown against my pussy. "Please," I said. "*Please*."

"Please what, wildcat?" His voice wasn't teasing, it was demanding. He wanted to hear me say how much I wanted this, wanted *him*, and I didn't deny him.

"Please...I want you inside of me."

"You want me to fuck you?"

I didn't hesitate. "Yes." And then he inched himself inside, ever so slightly, no more than he had been two nights before.

"Look me in the eyes," he ordered. I tilted my head up, immediately caught up in his gaze. There was lust there, but there was something else too, and my heart thrilled at the sight of it. I had never allowed myself to think that Mr. Markham would feel anything for me but sexual desire, but right now, at this moment, I thought I saw something more. Something softer and deeper.

I smiled up at him, and he bent down and took my mouth in a savage kiss, as if my smile was something to be adored and punished at the same time. He pulled up. "Watch me," he demanded. "Watch this."

And then he pushed himself all the way inside, pushing past that initial point of resistance, and I gasped at the sharp and unexpected pain.

His hand found mine. "Do you need to stop?"

I shook my head. There was so much pressure,

so much fullness, but also so much pleasure laced through it all, and I didn't want him to stop.

He went slowly, and even though I was so aroused, so wet, there was still some discomfort as he slid in and out. He groaned, his hands knotted in the coverlet by my head, as if he were straining to go so slowly. "You are so fucking tight," he said. There was something like a threat in his voice, the threat that he wouldn't be able to hold on to this uncharacteristic tenderness much longer.

He ducked his head down to suck on my breasts, his movements still careful and slow. And then he reached down and stroked my bud, softly, lightly. The sudden rush of sensation, of sheer pleasure, made me shudder, and Julian groaned again as he felt me quiver underneath him.

"Tell me," he said huskily. "Tell me what it feels like."

"I feel so... *full*," I whispered. There was no other word for it. He filled me and stretched me, and every time he moved, delight and pain spiked through me. "But at the same time, I want more. More of this. More of you."

He angled his hips upward, and he brushed against a spot inside of me that made me whimper. "You have all of me, Miss Leavold." He started moving faster now, his cock hitting that place over and over, and his thumb still making expert circles over my clitoris. The pain subsided, and all that was left was pleasure, pleasure so deep, so intense, that it barely compared to anything I'd felt before at his

149

touch. This was terrifying and transformative, deep and wild, and I realized I was moving under him, becoming more and more desperate with each stroke.

"Oh," I breathed. "Oh, please…"

He looked down at me, hair spilling across the pillow, my back arching and my legs opening, and I saw the darkness unfurling in his eyes. "I want to feel you come around my cock," he said. "I want to feel you clenching around me."

My body responded to his command, tensing tighter and tighter, and when I looked down at us, at him moving in and out of me, at our legs tangled together, at how exposed I was, how vulnerable and wanton I was at the same time—I came once more, an orgasm more powerful than any I'd ever felt, shuddering and tugging down to my very core.

"That's it," he said. And then: "Forgive me."

With his knees, he nudged my legs farther apart and drove into me. I cried out—half in rapture, half in pain—the waves of my orgasm leaving me impossibly sensitive, and he met my eyes. There was no tenderness there, no checking in to see how I was faring, there was only lust and raw desire. Only shadows.

"I wanted you from the moment I saw you," he growled as he thrust into me viciously, repeatedly. "I wanted you like this, your virgin cunt mine and mine alone. I wanted to feel you come around me. I wanted to come deep inside you, to mark you as *mine*."

How could he not know? "I *am* yours, Julian."

As he crushed his lips to mine, I felt his whole body stiffen. He groaned into my mouth as he filled me with his heat, pulsing and throbbing, and the sound of his breath as he came was the most beautiful thing I had ever heard.

We lay there, his body heavy on mine, his face buried in my neck. I ran my fingers through his thick hair, feeling a happiness that I had never felt before. I had often felt the untamed peace of swimming and climbing, and the gratification of a good book and a quiet room. But this feeling—it was fragile and floating, unmoored from all practicality, all the things that I knew to be true about men and men with money. Unmoored from my fierce desire for independence and liberty. I loved Mr. Markham, and now he was here, in my arms, and I could easily let myself believe that was enough.

Chapter Fourteen

After a long minute, he stood and pulled on his trousers. Without asking, he lifted me in his arms again, setting me down on a chair near the fire, then going to his washing table and wetting a linen towel. He came back and knelt in front of me, gently parting my legs. Slowly, he began cleaning me, starting with my inner thighs and working his way to my center, and when he pulled the towel away, I saw that it was tinged pink.

I had bled; it was a moment that was supposed to be reserved for my wedding night, but I didn't care. I knew no wedding night awaited an impoverished orphan—at least not a wedding night with a man I truly wished to be with. But despite the transgressive nature of tonight, the shock of the blood and its confirmation that it all had been real—I still felt that fragile happiness. And no bridegroom had ever been tenderer to his bride than Mr. Markham was to me in this moment.

The towel was soft and cool against my skin, and when he finished, I almost asked him to keep going. Instead, I waited as he brought me his dressing gown, a heavy thing of gold and crimson brocade, trimmed with velvet. As I stood to pull it over my shoulders, to tie the sash around the pleated folds, a knock sounded at the door. I cast my eyes around, desperate for a place to hide—I'm sure Mr. Markham didn't want the servants to know what he was doing with his dead wife's cousin.

"Have a seat, Miss Leavold. I assure you, my servants are very discreet."

I doubted that, but I was also buoyed by the fact that Mr. Markham wasn't ashamed to have it known that I was in his chambers. He wasn't ashamed of me.

The door opened and Gareth stood outside. "Sir, I hate to bother you this late, but—" His eyes lit on me, wrapped in the dressing gown, my hair tousled and my face undoubtedly flushed. Something moved under his expression—jealousy? judgment?—but whatever it was had vanished before I could properly assess it.

"There's a problem," he continued, studiously avoiding me. "One of the horses has escaped from the stables."

"What do you mean, escaped?" Mr. Markham demanded. "Which horse was it?"

"Yours, sir. Raven." Gareth sounded genuinely regretful. Horses were expensive, and beyond that, I knew that Mr. Markham treasured Raven and rode him whenever he had the chance. And, I remembered from that long ago conversation with Gareth by the dry stone wall, it was the horse that had killed Violet.

"How could you let such a thing happen?" The man who had so tenderly washed me was gone, replaced by the furious landowner I now saw. The muscles in his back and shoulders tensed, and for a moment, I thought he was going to strike something or throw something or shout, but his hands balled at his sides and he mastered his anger. "I'll come at once."

He didn't look at me as he grabbed his shirt and jacket, and he didn't say a word in farewell as he left.

I was completely alone.

For several moments, I sat utterly still, letting the events of the past hour soak into me, unable to process how everything had happened so fast, how I'd awoken a virgin and now found myself naked and alone in Mr. Markham's rooms. It all seemed so hazy and unreal, like a dream half-forgotten upon waking, but the raw ache between my legs testified how actual tonight had been. I'd done it, done the only thing I'd wanted to do since I'd met Mr. Markham—and the one thing an unwed lady should never do.

But, of course, that bothered me very little. I had no potential marriage to throw away. In fact, since my sole means of survival were currently in the hands of Mr. Markham, perhaps giving him myself was the best thing I could do for my future. I stood, a smile playing on the edges of my lips as I allowed myself to fantasize about a future with Mr. Markham. The two of us, spending our days entwined here at Markham Hall, seeing and feeling and tasting nothing but each other.

Mr. Markham's rooms were quite large, in the traditional medieval way. A sitting room with a massive fireplace adjoined the bedchamber itself,

154

where the rumpled blankets and sheets told the story of what had happened there tonight. My pulse raced when I saw the small splotches of blood on the snowy linen...would Mrs. Brightmore guess?

She won't have to, I told myself. Gareth had seen me, and if anything was certain in this life, it was that servants loved to gossip. Soon the entire household would know that I'd let Mr. Markham have me, and while I didn't necessarily feel ashamed, I did bristle at the thought that they might now consider me weak-willed.

I found myself pacing, my euphoria now dampened, and as if one nervous thought spawned another, I found myself also wondering at Mr. Markham's departure. I knew he had to find his horse, obviously, but without even a word of goodbye?

A memory of a book floated to the surface of my mind, a novel about a woman who failed in her chastity and ultimately died of consumption. I remembered the character leaving her lover's rooms quietly after every assignation because it wasn't seemly for such women to presume upon a man's time. They had one purpose, one task, and once that was fulfilled, they only stayed at the explicit request of their paramour.

I pulled the dressing gown tighter around myself, suddenly wondering if I'd made an error, a gaffe that displayed my total ignorance of society. Should I have left immediately? Was Mr. Markham disgusted with me, bored with me, annoyed that I had lingered after the act?

Surely not. He had carried me from the bed, cleaned me and dressed me. These were idle frets...yet they seemed reluctant to wither away, the roots already finding purchase in my mind.

Besides, I had gone into this with my eyes open. I knew exactly what kind of arrangement this was. If I found myself being treated like a prostitute, well...what else could I have expected?

A picture on the mantle caught my eye. I stepped closer, taking it in my hands. It was a small oil painting of Mr. Markham in profile, very cunningly done and by someone with a lot of talent and training. I bit my lip when I saw the name at the corner—spiky and unmistakable.

Molly O'Flaherty.

She had painted this and given it to him. And he had displayed it prominently in his room. A swell of jealousy and the horrible recollection of hearing the two of them kissing—the knowledge that those had not been their first kisses, not even close—and all of a sudden, the giant room seemed too small, the velvet curtains too dark and the fire too hot. I went to the door and ran down the hallway to the stairs, consumed with a single thought: *outside.*

I pushed past doors and through rooms, and then I found myself in the garden outside, the stars glittering in the clear sky above. The moon was still high—it was not that late, despite the feeling that I had lived an entire lifetime since supper. If the houseguests had been here, the night's revelries would have only just begun. I had no shoes and only the dressing gown separating my skin from the night air, but I didn't care, and I knew the darkness would shroud me from the gazes of anyone who could watch.

I went down to the stream, trying not to think of Molly and her bright eyes, her shipping fortune, her wild history with Mr. Markham, and failing wildly. He had held her at a distance, he claimed he only wanted me, but then he had that picture in his room. She was so much better suited to him—already part of his circle and wealthy—not to mention that her charisma and vitality enchanted even me when she wished it to. Again, who was I to be jealous of her? I knew the dynamic of my relationship to Mr. Markham; I had no claim on him. It was illogical to feel possessive just because I'd been foolish enough to fall in love.

But, I argued with myself, he sometimes seemed as infatuated with me as I was with him. I knew I wasn't imagining that. He said so himself.

But then again, it wasn't a matter of interest or attraction. Molly herself had told me that. It was a matter of duration. How long until Mr. Markham grew tired of me and moved on—or worse, back to Molly? Would he allow me to continue living at his home? More importantly, would I be able to go on after losing him?

When I finally reached the water, I was near tears—tears that had so many causes and influences that I couldn't push them down or away—but I wasn't prone to crying, and so they remained on the edge of spilling over, burning my eyes and tightening my throat. I sat on a stone, my breathing erratic and forced, remembering all the other things that should have warned me away from the tortured man who had accepted responsibility for my life. Wispel's words, Mrs. Harold's words, Gareth's words. Even his own words.

They said he murdered Violet. That he possibly murdered his first wife.

Was I in danger of more than having my heart broken?

The night brought no answers, no comforts, except that my restlessness and confusion had enough space to breathe. I paced the moonlit path by the stream; I swam; I tried to rest in the grass, but peace was elusive. I couldn't go back to the house—not now. I couldn't face his empty bed—or mine. Instead, I listened to the owls and bats flapping through the dark, to badgers and foxes rustling through the woods, to the water spilling its eternally cheerful spill.

Perhaps these doubts were galvanizing. They were all pointing to something—that either my heart or my life were in danger, and that perhaps I should leave. But where? I would have to search for employment, and at that, I balked. Being a governess was the most respectable thing I could think of, but to be shackled to the caprices of a wealthy family, my time no longer my own...

And I didn't want to leave Mr. Markham and his dark, somber house. No matter how bad he was for me, I couldn't truly fathom extricating myself from him. I craved him too much.

The sky darkened and lightened, finally blushing slightly at the edges of the horizon, and I decided that I should go back up to the house. I was cold and stiff and weary, and there were no answers out here. Only more doubts.

As I took to the path once again, I heard footsteps. I froze, my mind flashing to old stories of highwaymen and ghosts, but it was Mr. Markham who emerged out of the gloom, breathless as if he'd been running.

"Oh thank God," he said hoarsely, coming to me and drawing me fiercely into his arms. "I thought you'd left. Oh God, I thought you'd left."

There was ragged desperation in his voice, and its intensity both thrilled and frightened me. "Where would I go?" I asked honestly. "This is the only home I have."

"Even so, I thought maybe I had driven you off, pushed you away by fucking you."

And before I could answer, he crushed his lips to mine, parting my mouth with his own, as if he was trying to claim my body once again with a kiss. His hand reached inside the dressing gown and he was palming my breast, my nipples growing hard against his touch, and then he was ripping the gown off of me, pushing me to the ground. He unfastened his trousers with one hand, lowering them just enough to free his member, which was already hard and ready.

I saw his face, saw the hunger in his eyes, and I knew that this was the darkness he had referred to, the possessive and unmerciful darkness that had disturbed Violet, and I knew that this time would not be gentle or tender. I should have been wary, scared even, but instead heat blossomed below my navel and my pulse raced. I wanted this—him, all of him, rough and hard. I wanted him to own my body and own me; I wanted him to claim it, and I had never wanted anything more.

He unceremoniously spread my legs and I felt the heat of him pressing against my pussy.

"Oh, please," I murmured, and that was all he needed. He pushed his way in, and despite the soreness, despite my unreadiness, my body responded, rising up to meet him. He pulled out to the tip and then thrust in again, hard, and I moaned.

"You are mine," he said as he began driving in faster. "You are completely mine. Only mine. Your cunt and your lips and your heart—they belong to me." The darkness in his words was underscored by something anguished, something desolate.

He drove into me, harder and harder, as if urgently trying to reassure himself that I was really here, that I was really his. Over and over again he buried himself, hitting that place inside that stoked such wild delight within me, and then he reached down to brush against my bud. It took mere seconds, and then I was seizing around him, crying out, the pain making the orgasm stronger and deeper, longer even, and I was still riding the choppy waves of it when he pulled out.

"I thought you had left," he whispered. His cock glistened in the dim light, and it only took one stroke of his hand before he spilled himself, long spurts lacing my skin as he ejaculated onto my belly and onto my wet cunt.

We breathed there for a moment, breathing with the trees and the water and the coming dawn. The lust didn't bank in his eyes as he gazed at me, naked with leaves in my hair, his seed marking my skin. Indeed, his cock stayed mostly erect as he picked me up and carried me into the stream, where he washed me once more, and then fucked me in the summer-warmed water until my cries stirred the forest leaves.

Chapter Fifteen

I slept most of the day, in my own bed, since Mr. Markham had to attend to a problem on a tenant's farm. When I emerged, the late afternoon sun was beginning to sink and the smells of dinner wafted through the halls. I dressed—one of my old ones, since I felt strange donning one of the new ones if I was to be alone for dinner—and walked downstairs, passing Mrs. Brightmore carrying a hamper.

It was full of the sheets from Mr. Markham's room. I flushed and looked down, hoping that we would continue in our habit of not addressing one another, but I heard a muttered word as I passed.

"*Slut.*"

Now I flushed for a different reason, anger pulling at every part of me. "What your master does in the privacy of his own room is none of your business."

She turned to me, harsh lines around her mouth. "You are not the first, you know. And you won't be the last. He was wild before he married Arabella and he's been wild ever since. You are nothing to him but a way to pass the time."

The fury that rolled through me was all the stronger for the fear that birthed it. "I wouldn't expect you to know anything of how he feels."

"You think so?" She stepped closer to me, and once again I realized how young she was, younger than her bearing and plain clothes made her appear. "I've worked in this house for years. He handpicked me from another house because he was so impressed with me. You think that you—a charity case—can do any better than his late wives, both beautiful and wealthy? And even they could not capture his heart. He is destined for someone better. I've always known it. Better than that whore, Violet Leavold, and better than *you*."

It was in the way that she said it, the way that her shoulders straightened and her chin lifted, that I realized the truth. "You're in love with him."

"Don't be ridiculous," she snapped.

I didn't answer. I didn't need to. The heart of her spite had been laid bare, and we both knew it. I turned away from her and walked away, wanting to rage at her, to scorn her, to strike her, and knowing that none of these things would be helpful to me or Mr. Markham. And I couldn't scorn her.

How could I, when I wasn't entirely sure my own love wasn't as hopelessly misplaced as hers?

"You'll be gone soon enough," she called after me. "Just like the late Mrs. Markham!"

I went to the library.

I went outside.

I wandered through the garden.

But still agitation stabbed through me, relentless slices of doubt and worry and suspicion. Would it always be like this, loving Mr. Markham? Passion and fear, laced together, one chasing the other until it was impossible to tell where one started and the other began?

I couldn't articulate to myself why Mrs. Brightmore's words ate away at me, after the pleasure of last night and after the genuine need for me I'd seen in him this morning. After I had told myself that I *trusted* him, that I *didn't care* about the strange circumstances around Violet's death. That I would throw away that tiny chance at a future away from Markham Hall to live however long I could in Mr. Markham's bed.

But eat away at me they did. Maybe it was the certainty in her tone. Or the blazing conviction in her eyes. She felt so sure that I'd be tossed aside like so much rubbish.

Or was she sure that I would be dead?

Despite the warmth in the garden, I felt chilled to the core. I couldn't endure this any longer, the way Violet's death hung around Markham Hall like a poisonous fog. I had to find out the truth. Had to.

My wanderings had taken me to the front gate of the property, where I stood looking out onto the road to Stokeleigh, and a faint idea substantiated itself. Without giving myself time to thoroughly canvass the wisdom of my plan, I set off for the village, hoping that the policeman who'd investigated Violet's death would be readily found.

It only took fifteen minutes for me to reach the village, by which time moisture had dampened my brow and my hair grown a little disheveled from the summer wind. I stood at the head of the high street, wondering where I should go and whom I should talk to, when—inevitably—I was approached by Mrs. Harold.

"Miss Leavold! What a surprise!"

I squinted at her in the sunlight. She only had one of her retinue trailing behind her, and her arms were full of flowers.

"I was picking flowers for the altar," she explained. "Would you walk with me there? It's only a short way."

Of course, I didn't want to. The rector's wife irritated me beyond measure...*but.* A single thought prevented my instinctive refusal of her offer: she was the most well-informed person I'd met thus far, well-informed *and* willing to share her hoarded information. If I wanted to find the policeman who'd carried out the murder inquiry, Mrs. Harold would know his name, location, family history, and current medical ailments.

"I'd love to walk with you," I said and I meant it.

Three hours later and I was outside the North Riding of Yorkshire police building in Scarborough. I had walked the ten miles by myself rather than taking a horse or asking Gareth to hook up the phaeton for me. I didn't want anyone to know about this errand—especially not anyone who might feel duty-bound to report it to Mr. Markham. But as I pushed my way across the busy sea-scented street, I felt a tug of uncertainty. Would it be inappropriate for me to show up unannounced? I was hardly familiar with how these things worked—perhaps most people wrote letters to inquire about these sort of things rather than visit in person. Or they had a solicitor or agent inquire for them.

But, I reflected as I smoothed my hair and dress, I was Violet's only living family. I had the right to ask around, the right to know what happened. Surely, my familial connection to the victim would cover over any irregularities in my approach?

The building was nondescript, a small brick affair, and I was met with an industrious—if gloomy—interior. A man was crossing the foyer when I entered, a hat tucked under his arm.

"May I be of service?" he asked, seeming to want to be anything but.

"I'm looking for Officer Mayhew," I said.

The man blew out a breath then gestured for me to follow him further into the murk. Far-spaced windows weakly illuminated several desks, all covered in papers, and corridors leading down even darker halls. Tobacco smoke overwhelmed me, making my eyes sting, and I didn't realize that the man had stopped until I very nearly ran into him.

"A lady for you, Mayhew," he said and then departed without any further pleasantries.

Mayhew grunted but didn't look up for a moment, his hand jotting notations as he peered at barely legible list—a shop inventory it looked like.

I sat without being invited to, and he finally looked up, surprised. I don't think the man's introduction had even registered with him. He was

166

handsome, much younger than I expected, perhaps the age Thomas would be if he were still alive. Reddish hair and grayish eyes, a strong and determined mouth.

"I apologize, Miss—"

"Leavold," I supplied.

"—Leavold," he said slowly, memory filtering in through his eyes. "I didn't notice you. How may I help today?"

I didn't see any point in dancing around the subject. "My cousin died two months ago, Mr. Mayhew. I would like to know more about the circumstances surrounding her death. Her name was Violet Markham—nee Leavold—and she was married to Julian Markham of Markham Hall."

He looked at me a long moment, a look of consideration and calculation, and finally he released a long sigh. "I'll be back in just a moment," he said, standing and leaving his desk. True to his word, he was only gone for a few minutes, returning with a thin sheaf of papers bound with twine.

"I'm afraid I can't tell you much," he said, slicing the twine cleanly with a small knife. "Because I learned very little in my investigation. And if the investigation were not closed, I would not be able to divulge even that much. But since it is finished and since you are the only kin of hers that has come forward to inquire…" As he talked, he disseminated his bundle in small, precise piles around his desk. The papers now appeared group by content—or by date. It was difficult to decipher the handwritten words upside down. He looked me once more in the eye. "What do you already know?"

"That she was killed in the early hours of the morning. Thrown from her horse. That Mr. Markham was purported to be the first to find her, but that there were other footprints in the frost..."

A thick piece of paper was presented to me as I said this. It took me a moment and several rotations of the paper to make out what I was looking at. "It's the sketch of a footprint," I said.

"Yes. April can be, for all its chilly nights, quite mild during the day. A servant had come from Markham Hall very early to tell us that Mrs. Markham was missing. By the time the police had come, she was dead, obviously, and the frost had mostly melted off the grass. Mr. Markham told us of the tracks, that he was certain another party had found his wife before he did. We found nothing until an officer, working to find the horse's prints, found a spot of half-fading frost under a nearby bush. There we found a vague footprint along with other marks that suggested someone had knelt there before they stood."

I tilted the paper again. "It looks quite large," I said. "It must be a man's."

"I agree. It is nearly the same length as my own feet. But do you see how pointed it is at the top? How distinct that point is! Mr. Markham owned no shoes with such a point, although that in and of itself isn't such solid evidence. He would have had plenty of time to hide or even burn a pair of shoes if he wanted, before the police arrived."

It didn't fit with my image of Mr. Markham at all, a hunched man furtively feeding a pair of shoes into the fire. And I had seen his eyes and his face, had heard his voice when he told me about finding Violet that fateful morning. No. I believed Mr. Markham on this point at least. The print belonged to someone else.

Another sketch was passed to me, this time of the saddle. I studied it for a moment. "Yes," I murmured. "It does look as if someone cut it."

"They cut a little more than halfway through the cinch itself. And they would have known Mrs. Markham to be quite a vigorous horsewoman—everyone knew it. She had only crossed half the field behind the stables before the saddle failed and she was thrown."

I set the sketch down, banishing the image of her body tumbling from the horse, trying to unimagine the sound of a scream cut short. "Mr. Mayhew, do you have any reason to believe that Mr. Markham killed my cousin? That seems to be the popular opinion in Stokeleigh and beyond, yet he wasn't charged with the murder, so how complete can his guilt truly be?" I sounded like I was trying to convince myself, not ask a genuine question. I cleared my throat. "I would like to know, for Violet's sake."

Mr. Mayhew plucked at the corners of the paper stack in front of him. "That's not an easy question to answer, Miss Leavold. They were heard fighting

169

viciously the night before her death—"

"By the rector's wife?"

"—by an entire dinner party of people. Her relative unhappiness seemed to be well-known. And..." he seemed reluctant to speak whatever he was thinking out loud, handing me another paper instead.

I scanned through it. It took me a moment to realize it was the coroner's description of Violet—or of her dead body. Clinical descriptions of her twisted neck, of her skin otherwise unmarred, of her early state of—

I gasped.

I reread.

No, it was impossible even on a second inspection. It could not be true.

My heart pounded. "Was he—is he—the coroner, I mean, is he quite certain?"

Mr. Mayhew slid the paper out of my trembling fingers. "I do not want to trouble you with the particulars of his often gruesome vocation, but yes— he was entirely sure. His best estimates put the age of the fetus at somewhere between two to three months—closer to three, he felt."

Nausea coiled in my stomach and I was suddenly very glad that Mr. Mayhew didn't allow me to read further, to flip over to the penciled drawings on the back.

"You must compare the dates of the pregnancy with her marriage to Mr. Markham," he said, neatly stacking the papers. "The child was clearly conceived before the wedding ceremony. Not as unusual as people often suppose, perhaps, save for that Violet Markham was known in London for— pardon my boldness here—being at times too fond of the company of the opposite sex. Even though she and Mr. Markham were engaged to be married, he may have had reason to believe the child was not his own. I've seen one or two men driven to passionate violence at the discovery of ordinary infidelity. But I have seen many, many more fly into a fury when they realize their wife carries another's child.

"So," he continued, his voice almost bland with professionalism, "do I believe Mr. Markham killed his wife and the fetus inside of her? Personally, I do."

Dread nestled against the nausea. I didn't speak, trying to master my thoughts, which presently fled from any semblance of order.

"However, there was not enough evidence to lay the charge at his feet. The fighting, the pregnancy, his placement at the scene of her death— to me it speaks of certain guilt. But where is the knife that cut the saddle? Where is the witness to him doing it? And what of this lone footprint that seems to corroborate his version of events? He is a powerful man in this county, Miss Leavold, and the person who accused him of murder would have to have more than instincts to call to his aid in a courtroom. Would you like a glass of water? You look pale."

I knew I must be pale; it felt as if all of the

blood in my body was pouring out of my heart and on to the floor. A baby. There had been a baby. That was heartbreak enough. And then to hear Mr. Mayhew's calm, experienced voice laying out his interpretation of the facts so precisely...

It's only his interpretation, I told myself. *He doesn't know Mr. Markham like you do—he hasn't seen how lonely he is, how tender he can be.* But I couldn't find it in myself to give those words the credence they needed to ring true. I didn't know what to believe about Violet's death or what to believe about Mr. Markham.

And yet I was still in love with him.

When I got back to Markham Hall, I took a small dinner of soup and bread in the parlor, and then retired to the library, too restless to sleep and too agitated to lie still. I tried to read, tried to focus my mind on anything other than Mr. Markham and the suspicions that surrounded him, but it was useless. Instead, I found myself staring at the small portrait of Arabella Markham. What sort of girl had she been? Quiet and shy? Or dainty and demanding? Had she known that she loved a future murderer? If gossip was to be believed, her *own* future murderer?

And if Mr. Markham *had* killed Violet, which Mr. Mayhew seemed certain of, had he known about the pregnancy? Was that his motivation or was it something else? Was the child his?

Without meaning to, I pressed my hands against my own stomach. Would I carry his child one day?

Could I be right now, at this very moment? And why, oh why, did that idea thrill me as much as it scared me?

I paced and paced, at turns furious with myself and terrified. How could I both love and desire a man accused of such evil? And what was this resistance to the very idea of not loving him? He could be passionate, brooding, forceful...*perhaps he was carried off in a fit of temper*, I tried to justify. *Perhaps she provoked him...*

The difficulty of it was that I wasn't sure if I was concerned about Violet's murder because I cared about the value of her life and her unborn child's. The concern emerged from a more selfish, a more ancient part of my mind—the one designated for self-preservation. Like a wolf catching the alien scent of lead and steel on the wind, like a rabbit catching sight of the fox, my very body trembled with the need to flee my hunter.

Or fight him.

Or fuck him, a dark voice whispered in my mind.

The problem was that I knew of very few prey who had the third reaction. So did that make me stupid? Or strong?

There was a knock at the door. Adrenaline surged through me, tensing my muscles and making my pulse race. I turned to see Gareth coming inside the room.

Gareth. Not Mr. Markham.

"Hello," I said, struggling to tamp down the

manic energy that now coursed through my veins.

"Miss Leavold," he said. "Do you need anything? More light perhaps?"

"A fire would be nice," I managed, "but only if it's no trouble."

"Of course not." He set to it right away, but his mannerisms were slow and thoughtful, as if he were trying to find a way to introduce a topic. I had no guess as to what that topic might be, and I didn't care. My thoughts only touched around three points: Mr. Markham, Violet, the baby.

Mr. Markham, Violet, the baby. Mr. Markham, Violet, the baby. Mr. Markham—

"I let Raven loose," Gareth blurted.

I stared at him as if he were speaking Icelandic. "What?"

"Raven. Last night. I was the one who let the horse out."

"Oh." Last night's events filtered through my thoughts, piercing the murk of fear and lust and doubt.

He was talking fast now. "I knew you had gone up to Mr. Markham's rooms, and I know what happened when his guests were here, I mean, I saw you on the parlor floor with them and their hands all over you, and I didn't know if you needed help or not. Although, I did know, because I know what kind of man my master is and I'm only sorry that I let the horse out too late—I had hoped to distract him and save you from his advances altogether."

It all finally processed—the fact that Gareth had

174

seen me while I had been laid so intimately bare the night I played Blind Man's Buff, his misguided help, the risk he had taken in order to "save" me. I almost wanted to laugh at the absurdity of it in the face of what I had learned from Mr. Mayhew today. Who could care about saving my maidenhead when my very life was at stake?

But it would not do to be so blunt, Thomas would say. "Gareth, you shouldn't have."

"It was worth it," he said. "I...I wasn't able to help Violet. I wanted to help you."

Oh. That put a different frame on things. I wished that he had been able to help Violet too.

I searched for a way to explain myself without sounding ungrateful. "Gareth, I wasn't coerced into anything by Mr. Markham. I wanted to be in his rooms. I wanted to be on the parlor floor. I asked for all of that."

Realization dawned on his face, and he turned back to the stacked logs, face aflame. "Oh."

"Thank you—"

"No, no, I understand," he mumbled, standing up. Fire now crackled on the andiron, making his fair hair orange. "My mistake."

"I do appreciate the sentiment," I said, a little pleadingly. I didn't want to lose his goodwill when I had so little of it in this new life of mine.

He nodded. "It was nothing," he said, eyes still downcast, and then he left.

Frustrated, I turned back to Arabella's portrait, angry with Gareth and angry with myself and angry with Mr. Markham. Why had Gareth done something so presumptive? So potentially employment-threatening? He seemed so good-natured that I hadn't thought of him as the compulsive type. And all for the memory of his master's dead wife?

And—selfish as I knew it was to think—how could anybody expect me to exhibit gratitude now? Tonight? When all I wanted to do was roar and slash and howl, to run until I was insensate to everything except the breath stinging in and out of my lungs?

"Ivy."

The sound took all of the air out of the room. I had no idea how long Mr. Markham been standing there and watching me think my half-crazed thoughts. But before I could ask or explain, he'd crossed the room and pressed his lips to mine.

"Every time I find you in my house, I have this desperate fear that it will be the last," he said in between kisses. "How can I keep a wild animal caged in such a forlorn pen?"

Wild. Yes. I was wild. And that very wildness urged me to push him away. He would be the death of me, he had killed Violet...

He moved his lips to my neck, and that voice perished as suddenly as it had arisen. Want kindled within me, and God help me if the fear did not make the desire all the sharper. God help me if the danger did not ignite additional layers of excitement in my chest, and when his lips finally met mine again with

176

the hunger of a starving man, the prey within me crowed at conquering the predator.

His lips on my skin were arousing, keenly thrilling, but at the same time, the most natural thing in the world. He and I were meant to touch each other, caress each other. How could I fear the man I was made for? No matter what he had done?

As if reading my thoughts, he pulled away. "Ivy, we need to talk."

Trepidation coursed through me. It was a ridiculous fear given what I had learned today…but what if he told me that we couldn't continue on like this? I had expected him to abandon me at some point, all men did with their mistresses, but this was too soon, too, too soon.

I let him guide me to the sofa, and then he went over to a low bar to pour himself a glass of something dark and smoky-smelling. He handed me a glass too, which I accepted but did not drink. I felt wary, on edge. *Please don't let this end yet*, I prayed. *I need more of this. More of him.*

He sat next to me, tugging at his cravat. He still wore his traveling boots and he smelled of the summer evening—dry grass and sunlight and that indefinable male scent that always clung to him.

"I want you," he said after a minute. Relief swelled.

"You may have me anytime you like, sir."

"Sir?" He raised his eyebrows. "Have I frightened you or distanced you in some way?"

My mind flashed to the police station, to the

scribbled coroner's report. "No," I lied, "but—"

He held up his free hand. "No *sir* then, unless my cock is inside of you. Then you may call me whatever you like." He finally pulled his cravat loose and tossed it on the floor. "Do you remember the night we were in here together? When I made you come for the first time?"

Heat sank between my legs at the memory. "Yes," I said, breath threading through my voice.

"You remember all the things I said to you?"

Once we start, there will be no stopping. I'll have you in every room of this house, on every surface. I'll make you climax as often as it suits me, even if it's several times an hour for an entire night. I'll make you thrash underneath me and beg...

I nodded, biting my lip.

"I meant those things. I *am* sorry that I couldn't stop myself from taking you..." His eyes trailed down my body. "But I'm not a saint, Ivy. And you are truly so delicious."

The heat was flaring now, spreading to my breasts, to every part of my sex.

"I want to show you how to please me and how I can please you. I would like to teach you how women and men are with one another. But first, we must talk about your position within my household."

My position. As a poor nobody. A thought of Molly and her reputed wealth wormed through my mind, but I forced myself to ignore it. All I had left in this world was my freedom and my pride; I'd sacrifice neither, not even for Mr. Markham. If he

178

meant to imply that I would be some sort of concubine, that I should use my body to earn my keep, then I would stand up and walk out. I knew there would necessarily be gray areas in our new arrangement, but my pride couldn't bear the idea of something as bald as prostitution. I'd rather be a governess than a strumpet.

I raised my chin, meeting his gaze, and he must have seen some of the conflict in my eyes, because he shook his head and said, "No, wildcat. That's not what I meant."

"Good," I said. "I won't be your whore simply because I have no money and no relations."

"This is exactly why I wanted to talk about this," he said, leaning forward. "Don't feel for a moment that I care about your status. In fact, I rather like having you here like this—all to myself and unattached to anybody else." The words were dark, the meaning darker. I shivered. He liked having me entirely at his mercy and his whims. And I liked it too.

He took a sip of his drink and then set it down on the table next to the sofa. "But I have to know that you aren't acquiescing to this out of fear or worry for your survival. There's no *quid pro quo* in my bed. I don't want that. I don't want you to want that."

I breathed again, my fists unclenching. I hadn't even realized that they were clenched in the first place.

He put his hand on my thigh, and instantly, my

anxiety and anger flooded away, replaced with desire. "I want to educate you, wildcat, not use you."

"So how do we go forward?" I asked. "I don't know how this works. Do we live as we do now and keep my...education...a secret? Or am I to be more like a mistress?"

Here his face set. Time seemed to slow incrementally, everything half a beat too slow and drawn out, from the desultory crackle of the fire and languid throb of my pulse.

"Neither," Mr. Markham said. "I want you to be my wife."

Look for the second installment of Ivy and Julian's story in February 2015.

About the Author

Sierra Simone is a librarian who writes unabashedly sexy books with brains, beauty and big words. She lives with her hot cop husband and family in Kansas City. You can stalk her on Tumblr and Pinterest. You can also email her at thesierrasimone@gmail.com.

Acknowledgements

Thank you to my magnificently patient (and magnificently sexy) husband, who supported me while I crawled down the rabbit hole of taking on yet *more writing* on top of my day job. And thank you to my kids, for being adorable and also for letting Mommy write stories instead of playing Candyland for the 518th time.

To Laurelin Paige, my Chosen One, for immeasurable wisdom, help, mentoring, moping, plotting and writing codependency.

To Geneva Lee, my first critique partner, for always being a voice of reason...and realism. To Melanie Harlow and Kayti McGee, for happy hours and commiseration. To Tamara Mataya, not only for being hilarious, but for being the best editor a filthy girl like me could ask for. To the ladies of the Order, thank you for letting me be a delicate flower, and to the ladies of WrAHM, for Tom Hiddleston pictures and lots of bad words.

And thank *you*, reader, for taking a chance on my little book of corsets and dirty deeds.

Made in the USA
Las Vegas, NV
09 July 2024

92076390R00111